SEEDS OF TIME

For Meaghan Jean, the reader,
and for Audrey Jean, who read to both of us.

SEEDS OF TIME

kc dyer

A BOARDWALK BOOK
A MEMBER OF THE DUNDURN GROUP
TORONTO · OXFORD

Editor: Barry Jowett
Copy-Editor: Andrea Pruss
Design: Jennifer Scott
Printer: Webcom

National Library of Canada Cataloguing in Publication Data

Dyer, K. C
 Seeds of time / K.C. Dyer.

ISBN 1-55002-414-0

 I. Title.

PS8557.Y474S4 2002   jC813'.6   C2002-902281-9   PR9199.4.D94S4 2002

1   2   3   4   5   06   05   04   03   02

Canada

THE CANADA COUNCIL | LE CONSEIL DES ARTS
FOR THE ARTS | DU CANADA
SINCE 1957 | DEPUIS 1957

ONTARIO ARTS COUNCIL
CONSEIL DES ARTS DE L'ONTARIO

We acknowledge the support of the **Canada Council for the Arts** and the **Ontario Arts Council** for our publishing program. We also acknowledge the financial support of the **Government of Canada** through the **Book Publishing Industry Development Program** and **The Association for the Export of Canadian Books**, and the **Government of Ontario** through the **Ontario Book Publishers Tax Credit** program.

Printed and bound in Canada.♻   Printed on recycled paper.   www.dundurn.com

Dundurn Press
8 Market Street
Suite 200
Toronto, Ontario, Canada
M5E 1M6

Dundurn Press
73 Lime Walk
Headington, Oxford,
England
OX3 7AD

Dundurn Press
2250 Military Road
Tonawanda NY
U.S.A. 14150

A girl, a beginning, a terrible start,
A school guards a cliff, dark and old...
A brief gleam of brightness, a light in the dark,
Argument, friendship grown cold.
Some questions, a lesson, a taste of black death,
A strange shattered home on the shore,
Portraits and secrets, a bully bereft,
A sad tale never spoken before.
Mystery deep, contraband under rocks,
A surprise in the cliffs near the tide,
A journey, new terrors, a horrible shock,
A face old and new for a guide.
Ancient world with young eyes,
black and sick, plagued with fear,
Attempted kidnap, run or die.
Return and regret...
...Glyphs aglow, secret shared,
Travellers three, side by side.
Ainslie, a tour; and a call to the feast,
Chief of the Guard in his prime,
A traitor unveiled, a secret released,
A battle, two friends lost in time.
When hours mean days, a race must rule all,
Voices, the dark and the sea,
Return to the past. Who is safe? Who did fall?
A message, a life legacy.
One last long journey home...
... a fight on the shore,
Little hope for a life lost to crime,
A short talk in a cave, a new school is born,
Could the future hold more seeds of time...?

ACKNOWLEDGEMENTS

I owe an enormous debt of gratitude to the readers and writers in my life, for it is their encouragement that has made this book possible. Thanks to my friends Linda and David Horspool, Meghan Wray, Penny McDonald, and Deborah Anderson, and to Jim Cummings's class at Gleneagles School for the patient listening, discussion, and reading that went into making this book. I am grateful to the members of the CompuServe Literary Forum and the North Shore Writers' Association for their sharp eyes and warm guidance, and to the wonderful Canadian writers Marsha Skrypuch and Shelley Hrdlitschka for their generous and gracious support. Special thanks go out to Barry Jowett for his hard work and kind words. And thanks most of all to Meaghan and Peter for the unwavering love they give to their baggy-eyed mother, the midnight writer.

CHAPTER ONE

The wheels of the Volvo spat gravel as they pulled into what looked like a country lane.

"I hope this is the correct turn," Dr. Connor muttered. "They did say there wouldn't be a school sign." The only indication on the highway was a small notice reading PRIVATE ROAD. The road turned out to be a long, winding driveway into the school grounds. The breeze that had been blowing all morning stirred the green and wine-coloured leaves of the maples and cherries lining the drive, but the ornamental trees blocked out much of the view of the grounds.

Darrell felt a sudden sense of panic. "Mom, this place seems so weird. Wouldn't you rather have me with you this summer? I don't need to go to an art school over the summer break. I'll just bring my supplies and follow you around. What could be more inspirational to an artist than spending the summer in Europe?"

Dr. Connor shook her head firmly. "I'm sorry, Darrell. If this were a sightseeing trip or even a business trip with conventional hours I would love to have you with me." She gripped the wheel and glanced at Darrell. "I hate being away from you for any length of time, sweetheart."

Darrell pounded her fist on her knee, furious. "Don't call me sweetheart! That was Dad's name for me. I hate it when you call me that." Her hands were shaking, and she looked out the window, her eyes hot.

Dr. Connor bit her lip and then reached over and took Darrell's hand. "This symposium is run by Doctors Without Borders, Darrell. It's an intensive four-week session that involves surgical observations during the day and lectures at night. I just won't have any free time. Besides," she added, glancing sideways at Darrell's red face, "the last time we talked about this, you said you were ready to have some time on your own. School's been out for two weeks already, and we agreed that this summer school would be the perfect compromise." She rubbed Darrell's arm. "It's close to home, a chance to work on your favourite subject, and it's something to do away from your own school and, er, friends …" she finished lamely.

"That's just your way of saying that I no longer have any friends," Darrell said stonily. She yanked her arm out of her mother's grasp. "Some great friends they must have been to begin with, too."

Dr. Connor's face reddened. "Darrell, we can't change the past. You are angry, and you have a right to be. But don't blame your friends for not sticking around. After the accident, you lost something. I don't know what it is … your sense of humour, or something. You seem so angry all the time now. You've scared all your friends away."

Darrell stared furiously at her feet while her mother fished between the seats and pulled a pamphlet out from the pile of papers stuffed against the hand brake. Still watching the road, she held out the pamphlet.

"It's time for you to join the world again, Darrell. This camp is a chance to make some new friends. And you won't be entirely alone. Kate Clancy is going to be there, too."

Darrell looked sharply at her mother. "I haven't spoken to Kate since the accident, Mom. She probably doesn't even remember who I am."

Dr. Connor sighed. "Of course she remembers you, Darrell. When I ran into her mother at the hospital last month, she told me about this summer school. She said she was sending Kate and she thought you might be interested, too."

Darrell leaned back in her seat and rubbed the brace on her right leg absently.

"Why would Kate want to go to an art school over the summer? She hates art! She only loves computers. She's always carrying that laptop around with her. She even takes notes on it in school. There is nothing about an art school that she'd like."

A buzzing sound filled the car, and Dr. Connor reached over and flipped off her cell phone impatiently. "It's not just an art school, Darrell." She pointed to the pamphlet in Darrell's hand. "Look, I talked at great length to the principal last week, and it sounds like a fabulous place. I trust the judgment of Kate's mother. And remember," she added, "I'm only in Europe for a month. If you really hate the place, I'll come and get you as soon as I get back. You can spend the rest of August at home when I go back to work."

Darrell sighed. She stuck her charcoal pencil behind her ear and craned her neck to see through the trees. Her drawing pad lay cast aside on the car seat, a half-completed landscape on the open page. A large backpack sat on the floor of the front seat, jammed full of art supplies.

"This place seems like it's in the middle of nowhere," she complained. "I can't see anything except a lot of trees."

"Relax, Darrell, we're almost there. The school is supposed to be right on the water, so I'm sure there will be more than just trees to look at." Darrell's mother checked her watch impatiently. The car bounced along

11

a little faster than was strictly necessary, spewing gravel as they rounded the turns. They swept around a final, sharp corner and the buildings of Eagle Glen School emerged in front of them.

The driveway circled right up to the front door of a grey building, which appeared to be an old lodge surrounded by outbuildings of various shapes and sizes. Behind the buildings, a scant hundred metres of winding paths led down a series of bluffs to the beach. Darrell stepped out of the car and looked around, feeling wary. The quiet, with only the sounds of the wind and the surf, leant an air of desertion to the grounds of the school. She couldn't see any trace of human habitation. A small sign of painted iron, supported by two low posts, was the only indication they had indeed found Eagle Glen School.

In spite of the warm day, Darrell shivered as the wind murmured through the leaves. The sound of the waves on the shore resonated, though she stood more than a hundred metres away. Her mother stepped out of the car and, seemingly oblivious to the strange quiet, walked purposefully into the building. The grey, weathered door closed smoothly behind her, and Darrell stood alone.

She started to follow her mother inside but paused to have a look at her surroundings. The grounds of the school were long and narrow, clinging to the small flat area between the shore and the mountains that rose behind.

The buildings themselves seemed very old and were mostly of cedar, weathered silver and grey. The main building loomed in front of her. It was chiefly constructed of old, grey logs, chinked together tightly against the weather. Several annexes of different shapes and building materials had been added to the original structure over the years. Darrell knew from reading the registration pamphlet that the building itself had originally been a hunting lodge and had transformed through various incarnations into a tourist hostel, a church seminary, and even a hospital for a time. Of all the additions, the most interesting and strange were two round stone towers, one at each end of the school. The towers were a product of the building's era as a hospital during the First World War, and they gave quiet strength to the structure as it stood guard, overlooking the waters of the fjord.

Darrell jumped as a large raven cawed loudly. It fluttered down to sit near her on a tree branch, looking her over boldly with a bright, black eye. She looked back with some curiosity. She had never seen a raven of this tremendous size before. Darrell knew that mountain ravens were much bigger than the city crows she was used to, but this one must be the king of them all. She stared back at the raven until he spread his massive wings and, with two great thrusts, was gone, following the wind up into the mountains.

A movement at the corner of her eye interrupted her meditation, and she turned to see the front door opening. Darrell realized she had been holding her breath.

Her mother emerged with a tall, trimly dressed man who looked surprisingly like a painting Darrell had seen of Leonardo da Vinci as a young man: neatly clipped brown beard, balding head, clever eyes. The resemblance was remarkable.

Darrell smoothed her sweater and nervously tucked her windblown hair back into her ponytail.

The man stepped forward and, smiling warmly, proffered his hand.

"You must be Darrell," he said. "I'm Arthur Gill. Your mother has signed your registration papers."

"More like commitment papers," Darrell muttered, her lip curling.

Mr. Gill acted as though he had not heard Darrell's remark and continued. "I am the artist in residence at Eagle Glen this summer." He looked keenly at Darrell. "I have examined some of your work, and I am very pleased to finally meet the person behind the artistry."

Darrell didn't know quite how to reply.

"I'm sure you'll find the location of this school will inspire your muse," he said. Darrell looked questioningly at her mother, standing just behind the artist. Janice

Connor shrugged, and Arthur Gill continued smoothly. "Since orientation isn't until tomorrow, you may want to take some time to make yourself at home here. I will arrange for a staff member to show you around."

Carrying a bag in each hand, he turned toward the front doors.

"If you will just follow me," he said, "I'll show you to the main office." Darrell scooped up her backpack and, with a black glance at her mother, followed Arthur Gill's retreating back. As they reached the main building, Arthur Gill carefully set the bags to one side of the front door and gallantly swept it open for Darrell and her mother.

Clutching her backpack with its precious contents, Darrell led the way into the building that would be her home for the rest of the summer.

The following hour was a blur. Darrell and her mother found themselves swept through the dark interior of the building by a small, round woman named Louise Follett who worked in the office. Mrs. Follett, clearly uncomfortable with leaving the sanctuary of her orderly desk, fairly flew through the school, with Darrell and Dr. Connor in tow. Darrell's head was spinning, and the classrooms left little impression, until they arrived at the art studio.

It was located at the base of one of the round towers that Darrell had seen from outside. The room was large and completely encased in curved panes of leaded glass. The sun had slipped above the mountains behind the school, and the art studio was flooded with warm summer sunlight, glinting off the taps, brushes, easels, and other equipment that filled the room.

For the first time that day, Darrell felt her heart lift as she looked around delightedly, admiring the wide variety of art supplies.

"I'm afraid I don't know much about this studio," Mrs. Follett twittered. "I'm certainly more comfortable in the kitchens and the regular classrooms."

Janice Connor watched her daughter's face with a relieved smile. "Don't worry, Mrs. Follett," she said. "I'm sure Darrell will be able to find her way around this room without any difficulty at all."

After a few moments more in the wonderful studio, Mrs. Follett hustled Darrell and her mother quickly through the top floor dormitories and down to the office. She sat back in her chair with a sigh of satisfaction and, duty done with the premature arrivals, set happily to filing registration papers.

Dr. Connor reached her arm around Darrell's shoulders for a quick hug. "I'm afraid that I have to leave now, darling," she said, glancing at her watch. "I have a final patient to see this afternoon, and then I have to catch my plane this evening."

Darrell's happiness from the art studio evaporated. She looked morosely at her mother. "Bye," she said, without expression.

"Darrell, don't be like that! You saw the art studio. It's not going to be that bad, and if it is, I'll be home in a month. You can tough it out until then. We'll make some special time to be together in August, I promise."

Darrell opened her mouth to reply but stopped at the feel of a warm hand on her shoulder.

"Welcome to Eagle Glen, Darrell," said a quiet voice from the dark hall. "I am Professor Myrtle Tooth, principal of the school."

Darrell found herself shaking hands with a woman very near her own height, with iron-grey hair and clear green eyes.

Professor Tooth nodded at Darrell and turned to Dr. Connor. "I trust that Mrs. Follett has given you her specialty whirlwind tour of our campus?"

Dr. Connor laughed. "Yes, I think we saw everything we need to for now. Mrs. Follett said that Darrell's things have been sent up to her room and we had a good look around the building." She looked fondly at her still glowering daughter. "Darrell was especially impressed with the art studio."

Professor Myrtle Tooth smiled and looked straight into Darrell's eyes. Her voice held an unmistakable note of command, though she spoke quietly. "I'm sure you'll find this a very special place, Darrell. By the end of your stay here, you may even find the art studio is one of the *least* interesting elements of this school. There are many subjects to interest an enquiring mind at Eagle Glen."

Darrell looked puzzled, and her mother spoke up. "That may be true, Professor Tooth, but Darrell's greatest love is her artwork."

Myrtle Tooth, her eyes on Darrell, smiled. "Eagle Glen is a wonderful school, Dr. Connor, and many of our students have found their lives enriched in ways they never expected." She nodded goodbye, turned away, and walked into the office and through a door behind Mrs. Follett.

Darrell turned in fury to face her mother. "What was that all about, Mom? I don't want to be forced to take a bunch of subjects I'm not interested in. I have to do enough of that during the school year at home."

Janice headed out the front door and walked to her car with Darrell trailing behind her. "It's going to be okay, sweetie," she said. "Professor Tooth told me that the first day is spent touring the various courses offered, and after that you get to make your own choice as to the classes you want to take." She slid behind the wheel of her car. "I'll call you from Brussels tomorrow night and you can tell me all about it." Blowing a kiss that Darrell did not return, she pulled back out onto the driveway, pausing only to let another car drive in, and, with a spray of gravel, she was gone.

Angry with her mother and perplexed from the conversation with Professor Tooth, Darrell wandered down toward the ocean. The school stood on a sort of promontory close to the centre of a small bay that was scooped out of the larger fjord. Darrell could see a jagged row of rocks that formed the northern boundary of the bay. In the other direction, she could see a small lighthouse perched on a rocky outcrop. The path wound back and forth down the cliff side, bypassing large boulders as it made its way to the beach. When she reached the shore, Darrell decided to make for a small point that nestled inside the protection of the lighthouse to the south.

The waves lashed the shore, clouds scudded across the sky, and small whitecaps began to rise up further out in the ocean. The breeze lifted Darrell's brown hair and swirled around her legs as she turned to walk along the beach. Above the tide line, the ground was a mix of rock and sand, packed hard and made for walking. This part of the shore was curved and jagged, with small beaches butting up against the cliffs. Walking paths criss-crossed the cliffs above, brown scars through the salal and kinnikinnick that covered the ground and grew up the mountainsides.

Darrell wandered along the tide line around the small, curved beach and out to the point of land that formed to the south end. She walked carefully with a measured tread and skirted any of the rocks close to the edge that looked slippery.

It had been hard saying goodbye to her mother, even if she *was* completely infuriating. Darrell's face furrowed in concentration as she tried to think of any possible way to avoid staying at Eagle Glen. The tin-horn honking of Canada geese flying by pierced her consciousness. As she lifted her head to look at the birds she felt the warm sunlight on her face, and she straightened her shoulders.

"It may not be Europe," she muttered to herself, "but there *is* something interesting about this place." She scraped a stick along the sand and tried to think of the positives. A month would give her time to figure out why she had such a strange feeling about this school. And, in spite of the swirling wind and the sound of the waves now slapping the shore, it was so quiet here after the city. That had to be a good thing. The school and staff were oddly interesting, and the buildings and setting were beautiful. There was much she could draw here.

Looking out over the bay, Darrell's fingers itched for her sketchbook and charcoal, but she didn't want to go back where there were people just yet. Hard as it was saying goodbye to her mother, it was harder still being in the company of people whom she had never met. She hated the look that formed in their eyes: puzzlement, then dawning understanding and, inevitably, pity. It made her furious. She didn't need anyone's pity. She kicked a small pebble violently, sending it over the edge of the embankment and down into the water.

"Hey!" a voice yelled from below. Darrell was so startled that she jumped backwards. Her feet slipped out from under her and she fell to the ground with a thud. A barnacle painfully scraped her left leg below the hem of her capri pants.

A head popped over the edge of the embankment. The boy was snarling, and he held a large stone threateningly in his hand. "What you think you're doing?" he demanded. "You nearly hit me with that rock!"

With a rope in the other hand, he clambered with some difficulty up the side of the embankment. Darrell felt her stomach contract as she stood up. This boy was bigger and more athletic than she was, and he was clearly very angry. She glanced behind her to measure the distance back to the school. She was surprised by how far she had come. She definitely couldn't beat this guy in a foot race. She decided to tough it out.

"What are you doing with that?" she asked, warily eyeing the rock in his hand.

"Throwing it at you," he replied nastily, and did.

In spite of his point-blank range, either his aim was poor or he deliberately threw it badly, as the rock just grazed Darrell's shoulder and bounced down the embankment behind her. Her shoulder stinging, Darrell stared in disbelief as the boy picked up another rock. She started to back away, trying to keep her footing on the pebbly surface of the point.

The boy paused, leering. "Hold still," he commanded. Panic swept through her at the thought that this boy was deliberately going to hurt her.

"Wait a minute —" he drawled, looking her over lazily. "Well, well, well, what do we have here?" Quick as a whip he lashed the rock, this time with deadly accuracy. It hit her right leg with a crack and again bounced off the edge of the embankment. She flinched, but didn't move.

The boy, openly grinning, walked slowly toward Darrell. Anger began to wrap itself around the edges of the fear she felt, and she lifted her chin and stared stonily at him.

"What the hell do you think you're doing?" she spat. "I didn't mean to hit you with that rock. I didn't even know you were down there."

"Just giving you a taste of your own medicine," he said, still grinning. He bent down and secured the rope in his hand around a jagged piece of rock. Darrell continued to back away, afraid to take her eyes off him.

"You walk pretty well, for a cripple," he taunted. "Nice little plastic foot you've got there." Darrell's mouth dropped. "Let me give you a little advice, Gimpy. This spit is mine. I fish here, I crab here. Stay away from it, or I'll have to see how fast you can run when I throw a rock at your good leg."

"I have as much right to be here as you do, you moronic slug," Darrell snarled. "This is my school and my home for the summer." She remembered walking along the docks near her street in the city and a sudden thought struck her. "Let's see your license for that crab trap!"

She paused, noting with some satisfaction the scowl that had replaced the leer on his face.

"I bet you don't even have a license. So really," she added, "I have more right to be here than you have. Maybe *you* should be the one to get lost." She whirled around and hobbled off the little point and back to the more trustworthy footing on the beach. Behind her she heard glass breaking.

She turned, from the safety of the beach, and looked back. Two other boys had climbed from behind the embankment and stood next to her tormentor. He was gesturing with a piece of broken bottle, and his friends laughed.

KC DYER

"Hey, Gimpy!" he called. "Next time I see you, maybe we could use this to cut off your other leg!" His friends howled with laughter. They turned their backs on Darrell and climbed down the far side of the embankment. A moment later an engine roared to life, and Darrell could see the three speeding off in an old wooden dory loaded with crab traps. One of the boys waved, and the boat veered crazily before they straightened out and plunged into the rising whitecaps in the direction of a small island further down the coast.

Darrell turned and slowly made her way down the beach back toward the school, holding her head high and trying not to limp at all.

CHAPTER TWO

Darrell trudged back to the school, any pleasure from her walk on the beach stolen by the boy with the crab trap. She headed back toward the main building, thinking she should report the incident to someone in authority, but found the office closed and locked.

Darrell wandered through the school and found herself in the small back garden that faced the water. She spotted a gnarled arbutus tree clinging tenaciously above the bluffs that led down to the beach. Scrambling up the tree she discovered that her perch gave a panoramic view of the shoreline below.

I'll have to remember to climb this tree before I head down to the beach again. She took her time examining the whole stretch of beach below and decided that it was truly deserted, with no sign of the crab trappers anywhere.

Darrell climbed down from her perch and wandered slowly down the winding path.

She kicked off her sandals and walked barefoot along the shore near the water line. The water was just losing its spring chill and the long, shallow reach of sand that led to the shore warmed it further. The water felt lovely on her bare toes and swirled around the waterproof exterior of her prosthetic foot.

Might as well enjoy the rest of this day, she thought, with a frown. *It's the last one before the stupid summer classes start.*

She looked further along the beach. It was still deserted, except for a golden-coloured dog, digging on the distant end of the shore near the rocky cliffs. About halfway down the beach was a large stump, perched upright on its jagged root system. Darrell decided to walk to the driftwood stump and back as a way to stake her own claim to the beach and prove to herself that the morning's incident hadn't completely frightened her.

She approached the ancient stump and gazed at it thoughtfully. The stump stood straight up on its gnarled roots, its trunk pointing a thick, jagged finger toward the sky. As she got closer, it loomed large over her, quite the most massive tree stump she had ever seen.

Darrell walked around the remains of the giant tree and decided to stop and rest on one of the long roots that protruded from under the old tree.

She sat down on the root, all its rough edges rubbed smooth by the work of water and sand. The dog picked its way among the long logs littering the beach and came over to her. His golden coat looked unkempt, but his smile was friendly.

Without a sound, he stepped closer to her, tail wagging gently. He bent his head and snuffled her hand. She caught a glimpse of his collar, ragged and without a tag. The worn blue material was woven through with the word *Delaney*.

When he finished his thorough sniffing of her hand, he turned in a tight circle and sat beside her.

"Hey, Delaney," Darrell said aloud. "Thanks for keeping me company." The dog stared out to sea and, without glancing at her, gently leaned his head on her knee in silent companionship.

There has to be one good thing about this place, she thought desperately. *Maybe this Delaney dog could be it.* Aloud she said, "Who do you belong to, boy?" and felt his collar again for tags. Nothing. She checked his ears for tattoos, but there were no identifying marks. As she stood to walk back up the beach, he got up and followed her, tail still wagging gently.

In the distance she could see a couple of cars pulling up at the school. She felt a strange sort of relief, a sense that she was no longer the centre of everyone's attention now that other students were beginning to arrive.

"You'd better go home now, Delaney," she said quietly to the dog. "I have to go up and find my room." Delaney snuffled her fingers and then turned and trotted off along the beach. "I wonder where you belong," Darrell breathed to herself. "I hope you haven't got anything to do with those crab trappers." She pictured the snarling face that had burned its way into her brain earlier that day. A face that filled with venom could never own a dog as lovely as Delaney. She lost sight of the dog after he circled behind the massive stump on the beach, and with a sigh she turned and trudged up the winding path to the school.

Back at the school office, Mrs. Follett gave Darrell directions to her room on the third floor. "It's a lovely location, Darrell. Just perfect for a girl with an artistic eye." Darrell rolled her artistic eyes, but Mrs. Follett went on without noticing. "It's the last room on the north end of the building, so it doesn't get too hot in the summer. It is actually a part of the tower at that end, so the room is quite round on one wall. It faces the bay and you will have a view of the most magnificent sunsets, behind the mountains across the water."

"Do you know who my roommates will be?" Darrell asked, feigning unconcern.

"Oh yes, dear. Your mother requested that you room with Kate Clancy. And you have another girl in with you — Lily Kyushu. She's a swimmer, I believe. Lily will be arriving late tonight." Mrs. Follett put her head close to Darrell's and whispered conspiratorially. "These swimmers; I just can't understand them. They like to do the endurance practice here, you know. Swimming to the various islands and even over to Vancouver Island, some of them!" She clucked uncomprehendingly as she ruffled through a pile of papers.

Darrell thanked Mrs. Follett for the directions and wound her way through corridors and up stairways until she found her room. She stepped through the doorway and found Kate Clancy and her mother had already arrived. The two girls looked at each other awkwardly, and Kate blushed until her face was almost the same shade as her rusty hair.

"Hello, Kate. Hello, Mrs. Clancy," Darrell said in a tight voice. They stood for what seemed an eternity, staring uncomfortably at the floor. Finally, Mrs. Clancy broke the silence.

"I'll leave you two to get used to your room — I'll be down in the office filling out some final registration papers. But I'll be back to say goodbye in a short while, Kate." Kate looked at her mother, as if pleading with her to stay, but Mrs. Clancy turned and headed out the door.

Darrell strode over to the bed by the window, piled with her bags and backpack. She turned her back on Kate and began to organize her things methodically.

"Just because we know each other from school doesn't mean you've got to have anything to do with me here," Darrell said coldly, without looking at her roommate. "I'm perfectly all right on my own."

Kate's face was once again beet red, but this time she looked more angry than embarrassed. "I've tried to be friends with you, y'know, Darrell. You are just so unbelievably stubborn. Even when anybody offered to help carry your books at school you acted like it was an insult."

"It was an insult!" Darrell snapped, whirling around. "Just because I lost my foot doesn't mean I can't look after myself. I don't need anybody. So just leave me alone, okay?" She slammed down a pile of sketchbooks on the desk beside her bed.

"Fine with me." Kate piled an inordinate number of stuffed animals onto her bed and then turned back to Darrell. "Look, it's going to be a long summer. Let's just try to get along, okay?"

Darrell looked back at her, feeling cold and resolute. "I'll stay out of your way if you'll stay out of mine."

Kate sighed. "That's not what I meant!" she said with exasperation and punched her pillow into place. "But I guess it will have to do." They both turned back to their unpacking and a few moments later Kate slipped out of the room, leaving Darrell alone with her thoughts.

Dinner that night was quiet. Mrs. Follett directed Darrell to the dining hall — one of the strangely shaped annexes protruding behind the main building. All the teachers except Professor Tooth were present, seated at a single long table at one end of the hall. There were twelve early arrivals besides Darrell, sitting quietly in groups of two or three, casting hidden glances around the room. Since the formal welcome and opening of the school was not to take place until the following day, most students would not be arriving until later that night or early the next morning.

Information sheets for early arrivals were stacked on each table. With a glance at Kate, Darrell took a sheet and sat by herself at a table in the corner. From her spot, she looked through a small garden behind the building and out to a horizon where the sea met the sky over the raised hillocks of islands, pushing their turtle backs out of the water to watch the sunset.

Professor Myrtle Tooth did not appear at dinner, but Arthur Gill stood up to briefly welcome the students and to invite them to spend the next morning at a school orientation program to help prepare them for the classes that would start the following afternoon.

There were a few good-natured groans from the students, but almost everyone went directly to their rooms after dinner. Darrell dragged herself upstairs, disappointed and discouraged with her day.

Kate must have been feeling similarly discouraged, as she got ready for bed almost immediately. She turned off the lamp at her bedside table but sat propped up in bed with her notebook computer on her lap, tapping away, her faced bathed in the blue light of the screen. As Darrell undressed for bed, the door opened and someone bounded in and flipped on the light.

"Hi! I'm Lily!" the new girl squeaked. She threw a pile of swim gear on her bed and noisily began to organize flippers and pull-buoys, goggles and earplugs, talking all the while.

"I'm so excited to be here! I'm in the swimming program. Training begins in the morning and I just can't wait! This summer school is supposed to be the greatest for training endurance swimmers, and I know I'll be one of the best! I am so psyched. This is going to be my year, I can just feel it!"

Kate looked at Darrell and rolled her eyes. Lily continued to babble on, heedless of the glances passing between the other two girls. Finally, she paused for breath, and Darrell jumped in.

"Did you say the *pool*? I thought you practiced endurance swimming in the ocean."

Lily looked disdainfully at Darrell. "Of course we'll swim in the ocean! We just have to do it gradually, getting used to the temperature change. You don't expect me to swim to Vancouver Island tomorrow, do you? Of course not," she said, answering her own question before Darrell had time to speak. Nightgown in hand, she leapt out of the room toward the bathroom in the hall.

Kate whistled. "Whew! She's unbelievable!"

Darrell didn't have time to reply. Lily leapt back into the room, screwed earplugs firmly into her ears, and hopped into bed. "Goodnight!" she called out cheerfully and closed her eyes. In less than a minute, quiet snores were emanating from her shadowed bed.

Kate looked at the tiny lump that was Lily and shook her head. "I've read about people like her," she said darkly.

Darrell quietly took off her prosthesis and curled up in a tight ball on her bed, pulling her pillow over her head to block out the sound of Lily's snores and the light of Kate's computer. One of the walls of the bedroom formed a part of the outside wall of the north tower, and Darrell peeped out to see the moon rising over the mountains behind the school, distorted through a curved pane of leaded glass. She watched the moon make its way slowly above the crest of the mountains and move out into the open sky. Forgetting Kate and Lily, Darrell sat up in bed to get a better look at the reflection of the moon on the water. She pulled her drawing pad from the neat pile on her bedside table and began to sketch. In moments, the view from the window began to emerge on her page.

"What are you drawing?"

Startled, Darrell snapped out of her reverie and dropped her charcoal pencil. She saw that Kate had shut down her computer. "Nothing, really. The moon. The light on the water." Her voice faltered. "I ... I don't know. Nothing you'd be interested in, I'm sure."

"I *am* interested," said Kate, kindly. "Actually, this whole place interests me."

Darrell closed her sketchbook and peered at Kate in the dark. "What do you do on that computer all the time, anyway?"

Kate perked up. "Games, mostly, but quite a bit of programming. I'm actually interested in creating virtual reality games that will work over the Internet."

"Whatever that means," said Darrell sarcastically. She saw Kate stiffen and softened her tone. "I mean, it's just that I really don't know about any of that stuff. My world is kind of different from yours, I guess."

Kate looked surprised at the conversational tone that Darrell was taking but, eager to mend the rift between them, continued to talk. "This place is actually pretty amazing," she whispered from her bed in the corner. "Have you seen the computer room?"

Darrell thought back to her whirlwind tour of the school earlier. "I can't remember that much about it," she confessed.

"Well, they have every system I've ever heard of, Internet access, and a whole slew of things I've never seen anywhere but in *Wired* magazine. Flat screens, voice activated equipment, virtual reality resources. It's unbelievable for a school."

Darrell turned over in her bed and looked out at the dark, star-dappled sky. "Unbelievable is a good word for it," she said slowly. "I've never heard of equipment that up to date in a school, and a summer school at that. We certainly don't have it in the computer lab at our school in Vancouver."

Kate sat up. "My mother told me Professor Tooth has been running a private school in Europe for years and that Eagle Glen School is supposed to be an extension of some special philosophy she uses there."

Lily spoke up sleepily. "Will you two shut up? I'm really tired and I have early training tomorrow morning. Besides," she mumbled from deep in her pillow, "if you are talking about state-of-the-art equipment, you can't beat the swimming centre here."

"I've heard it's really small," said Kate.

Lily eyes snapped open, and she looked indignantly at Kate. "It is small, but it's well designed. And they say

35

the coaches are the best. There aren't many swimmers elite enough to train here, you know."

"I know, I know," said Kate impatiently.

"I heard Professor Tooth say that you were trying out for the Olympic team in the fall. Is that true?" asked Darrell.

Lily looked from Kate back to Darrell, and the anger in her face drained away. For the first time, she lowered her head with what appeared to be modesty. "I am going to try," she said quietly.

Kate looked abashed. "What's your event, Lily?"

"My best distance is the two hundred metre IM," Lily replied with enthusiasm. "I have to develop more strength in the fly, but the front and back are no problem, and the breast is a piece of cake!"

Kate blinked. "I understood about half of that," she muttered to Darrell.

As quickly as she had awoken, Lily turned over onto her side and the gentle snoring began again.

Darrell lay back in bed. It was now well past midnight, and the moon was setting behind the mountains in the west as she rolled over and drifted off to sleep.

CHAPTER THREE

The triple peal of a bell ringing through the building woke Darrell and Kate the next morning at seven o'clock. Lily was nowhere to be seen. A notice pinned on the inside of the bedroom door indicated that breakfast was to be served at 7:30 A.M. Checking her watch, Kate scrambled to get ready and ran out the door in minutes.

Darrell felt tired and depressed. She was in no mood to rush off to some boring school orientation. She showered, dressed, and, still barefoot, slowly headed downstairs. It was almost eight o'clock by the time she walked into the deserted dining hall. She found a large urn of coffee, poured a cup, and headed outside to complete her morning ritual. At the side of the school, an open door led to the kitchens. She avoided meeting anyone and walked barefoot to stand on a concrete stepping stone outside the kitchen door.

A beautiful summer day was in the making, but the sun had just risen over the mountains behind the school and the air was chill. Darrell stood and stared moodily out over the water. Out of habit, she glanced at her watch. The fragrance of the coffee drew her and she drank it slowly and then glanced at her watch again.

"Ten minutes," she muttered. "Not a bad start."

A voice snapped her out of her reverie. She almost dropped her coffee cup.

"Ten minutes? Would that be ten minutes late for Orientation?" Professor Tooth stood at the door to the kitchen, looking calmly at Darrell with her clear, green eyes. Darrell felt emotions warring on her face: guilt, anger, sorrow. Stubbornness won out.

"That's not what I meant," she said, belligerently. "You're right, I would be ten minutes late for orientation, if I were going. It's just that art classes aren't scheduled until this afternoon, so I hadn't planned to go until then." Professor Tooth raised her eyebrows, but remained silent.

Darrell felt uncomfortable. It was hard to have an argument with someone who refused to argue back. She tried again.

"This is just something I do every morning. It's … it's kind of like an endurance test."

Professor Tooth nodded. She gestured down at Darrell's bare foot, red with cold from standing on the concrete block, and spoke quietly.

"Are you punishing yourself for the loss of your foot, by trying to freeze the one remaining foot you have?"

Darrell frowned, and she could feel a deep crease form between her eyebrows. She had never had to explain this to anyone before, and she wasn't sure she wanted to, anyway.

"It's not that at all. It's just — well, I stand on the cold step to — just to prove I can do it — I guess," she finished lamely. She felt anger rise up inside her at having to explain something so private to a relative stranger. "Besides," she added, "it's personal, and I don't think it's any of your business." She lifted her chin and stared defiantly at Myrtle Tooth.

To her surprise, Professor Tooth laughed. "You're right, Darrell. The things that go on in your head are your own special business. But I am principal of this school, and it's my job to ensure that my students are not a danger to anyone, including themselves." She looked thoughtfully at Darrell, and then changed the subject. "I think you may want to investigate a few classes other than just those in the Art Studio, Darrell. I have a hunch that you may find answers to your questions in places you may least expect. Now, if you will excuse me, I have a lesson that begins at ten o'clock." She smiled kindly, but her green eyes bored into Darrell's. "It encompasses some art history that you may find ... enlightening. I hope you can make it."

She turned and disappeared through the door to the kitchen. Disturbed and puzzled, Darrell made her away around through the front doors and up the stairs to put on a pair of sandals. Perhaps Professor Tooth's history class might be interesting after all. Darrell shrugged. *At least it will fill the time before art starts this afternoon*, she thought, and, grabbing a pencil and some paper, she headed off to find the orientation group.

Professor Tooth's history lesson did prove compelling. Darrell had never attended a class quite like it before. History was supposed to be boring ... it always had been boring, in her experience. But at this school everything was different from what Darrell had come to expect.

Professor Tooth began the class by turning out the lights and gathering the students together on the cold floor. In her strong, quiet voice she started what sounded like a ghost story. The students were completely silent as Professor Tooth spoke. It was the story of the life of a young person in the Dark Ages. Darrell and the rest of the class listened spellbound to the story of a young man named Luke, who lived to be only nineteen before being struck down by the Black Plague that swept through Europe in the fourteenth century.

In the weird twilit classroom, Darrell closed her eyes and watched the pictures play inside her imagination.

The painful difficulty of everyday life, the continuous daily struggle to defeat death or at least to push that bleak hand away for another hour or another day …

The class concluded with an examination of some of the contemporary art of the fourteenth century. The paintings depicted images both matter-of-fact and gruesome, as death made its way, unimpeded, across Europe and Asia. The combination of Professor Tooth's words and the pictures made Darrell's fingers itch. The art class that followed allowed Darrell some relief, as she was able to spend a merry afternoon sketching corpses in various states of decomposition, plucked from her mind's eye after the morning's lesson.

She walked thoughtfully out of the school at five o'clock. After checking from the arbutus tree that the beach was deserted, she wound her way down the path through the cliffs to the shore below. The day had proven much more interesting than she had anticipated, and she needed some quiet time to think over the latest developments. Though the sun had shone for most of the day, around three o'clock it had clouded over, and now the sky was completely grey.

Darrell wandered down the beach, lost in thought. She'd spoken to her mother briefly on the phone before heading outside. Janice Connor had sounded busy but was clearly very worried about Darrell. Grudgingly, Darrell told her about the interesting classes, and her mother had hung up sounding like she felt a little better about leaving Darrell at Eagle Glen.

Darrell heard a bark and looked up, delighted, to see Delaney bounding toward her. All her cares forgotten, she dropped to her knees and buried her face in the fur behind Delaney's ears. He smelled comfortingly of salt and sea and healthy dog, and they played tug with a stick from the beach. Darrell felt her heart thump as she patted the dog. It was great to have a friend who was always so happy to see her. The only pet she'd ever cared for was her neighbour's cat, Norton, and he wasn't good for much more than a pat or two every day. After five cheerful minutes, she stood up and wandered toward the giant driftwood stump, Delaney happily wagging behind her.

The shattered stump towered high in front of her, balanced on its system of roots that snaked and crossed like locks of Medusa's hair. As she had seen on her first visit, the surface of the wood was worn and was in places rubbed to a satiny smoothness by the action of the waves. Up close, the wood was a surprise, riddled with tiny holes. Darrell remembered reading somewhere that holes in coastal wood like docks and wooden-hulled ships were wrought, not by worms, but by borer clams, which lived by tunnelling in and consuming the wood.

Darrell ran her hand across the pitted surface, tracing the intricate pattern within the wood. Maybe this old stump would give her the answer to why she was here this summer. She sighed. Maybe it was as simple as learning to marvel at a world that produced a tree this size that could be brought down and digested by a tiny clam.

Darrell looked down at Delaney as he snuffled with clear interest under the roots of the ancient tree.

"Lucky I have you, boy," she said. "You're a lot cuter than a wood-boring clam." Delaney had started to dig a hole at the base of the tree, where one of the roots pushed deep into the sand. She bent to ruffle the fur on his back, but he would not lift his head, even to acknowledge a pat.

"What have you got there, boy?" Darrell was curious. Delaney was digging frantically, in a spot where the sand was soft. Suddenly, with a bark and a wiggle, he vanished from view.

"Delaney! Come back here!" Darrell called, worried. No sign of the dog. She dropped to her knees and stared with some surprise at the hole into which Delaney had disappeared. Apart from the small bit of freshly dug sand, there was an established tunnel under the winding roots of the stump. Without a second thought, Darrell flopped to the ground and, with her stomach on the sand, wriggled into the tunnel after Delaney.

She found it a tight fit only for a moment and then the tunnel widened to allow her plenty of room to move. She could feel air circulating above her head and slowly stood upright. Delaney barked again and nuzzled her sandy hand.

Darrell found, to her surprise, that she could stand up inside without stooping. She looked up and could see the jagged top of the trunk high above, pointing to the sky. From inside the ancient log, the pounding of the surf grew distant. She stretched out a hand to find the inner wood was smooth, soft, and damp to the touch. There was a smell that she couldn't place; a whiff of old fires left burning to cinders, of smoke, of peace. Instinctively, Darrell pulled back her hand to look for the telltale mark of charcoal, but her skin was clean. She replaced her hand on the inner wall of the log, noticing for the first time the warmth of the wood, in spite of the fact that the sun no longer shone outside. The texture drew her, and she closed her eyes and laid one cheek against the smooth surface.

The sensation was startling. With her hand and face against the wood, she felt as though she could see, taste, and smell the history of the old tree. The sound of the surf beating the ocean rocks into sand on the shore gave an undertone, and with her ear against the inside of the old log she marvelled at the deep, dull beat of drums. The smell of wood smoke, the tang of salt on her tongue, and the steady, solid rhythm filled her senses.

Delaney settled on the soft sand as pictures rose unbidden behind her closed eyelids. Darkness, figures dancing, wisps of smoke, and licks of flame. She could smell the water more strongly now, or was it the scent of crab being boiled in pots over open fires? She felt the passage of time course from the ancient driftwood tree into her fingertips. She stood rapt, in the grey light within the ancient tree, lost in a world that existed long ago. She opened her eyes and smiled at Delaney, who thumped his tail gently. She wished she had brought her sketchbook to note down the mesmerizing images that filled her mind.

"We'll come back here again, Delaney," she whispered. She dropped to her knees to pat him and saw that he was curled up on a scrap of tattered towel. She looked around and saw what she had not noticed before, shreds of old bone and a few scraps of well-gnawed wood. A thought dawned, and she grinned.

"Delaney!" she whispered. "This is where you live, isn't it?"

Delaney smiled with his mouth open and thumped his tail on the sand. Turning his head, he sniffed at the tunnel and gave a gentle woof.

"Darrell? Are you in there? What are you doing?" A voice, filled with concern, echoed in through the tunnel. Darrell was startled, then suddenly angry. She had found a special place, and it was already being invaded. She recognized Kate's voice but did not want to share her discovery with anyone. She thought about not answering, and she stood very still.

Kate's voice took on a frantic note.

"Darrell, please answer me, if you can. Are you in there? Are you hurt?" Darrell stayed still and silent.

"I can't believe this!" Darrell could hear Kate talking to herself outside the tunnel. "I've got to go in there. Brodie said he saw her go in, but what if I get stuck, too? What good is it if we both die on this stupid beach?" And then, more loudly, "Darrell! Answer me!"

Darrell closed her eyes and crossed her fingers that Kate would just go away and give her a chance to hang on to her secret. Her heart dropped as she heard a scrabbling sound at the entrance to Delaney's tunnel. Frowning, she sat down and watched as Kate wriggled her way into the hollow tree.

Kate sat up and brushed the sand off her hands. As she looked around the inside of the hollow log, her face first showed relief at finding Darrell in one piece, then darkened. "Are you crazy? What d'you think you're doing? You scared me to death." Her hair was sticking straight up with perspiration and wet sand.

Darrell started to feel embarrassed, but she clung stubbornly to her anger. "I just wanted some private time on the beach. I followed this dog and he came in here. I think he's a stray and this must be his home. What are you doing spying on me, anyway?"

Kate sounded defensive. "Well, you nearly scared me to death. I've been looking for you for over an hour, and if Brodie hadn't spotted you crawling into this old log, who knows what might have happened?"

"Nothing would've happened," Darrell snapped, and then paused and softened her tone. "Why were you looking for me? And who is this Brodie guy, anyway?"

"That's not important — you'll meet him. I was looking for you because I have something to show you, but I don't know why I bothered." Kate still appeared furious. She stopped to catch her breath, and for the first time she looked around the inside of the hollow driftwood log. Delaney whined, and Kate dropped to her knees on the sand to pat him. Her anger evaporated, and she looked up at Darrell.

"It *is* pretty cool in here, isn't it? I can see why you followed this guy. He's a great dog." She ruffled Delaney's fur. Darrell nodded and crouched down beside Kate on the sand.

"A pretty smart dog, too. This is a great shelter, and tucked under this side of the tree he won't even get rained on. It seems like he's been living on his own out here for a long time." She paused, and added, "He must've belonged to somebody once, though."

She showed Kate the dog's collar. Kate nodded and got to her feet. "I'm sorry I invaded your private place with Delaney," she said quietly. "I can talk to you about what I wanted another time. It's pretty late, and I'm going back to get something to eat."

Darrell looked at her watch and made a decision. "I'm coming with you. I want to get some food to bring back for Delaney so he doesn't have to forage anymore." She looked pleadingly at Kate. "Please don't tell anyone about this place. At least, not until I figure out what I'm going to do about this dog."

Kate nodded and dropped to her knees to crawl out of the tunnel. Delaney thumped his tail, and Darrell gave him a last pat.

"I'll be back later with some food for you, boy," she promised. She held her hand above his head and said, "Stay!" He wriggled contentedly into the sand and dropped his head onto his front paws. Darrell scrambled out through the tunnel and hurried to catch up to Kate.

"Hey! Wait up." Darrell ran up behind Kate. "You didn't tell me what you wanted before."

Kate looked thoughtfully at Darrell. "Well, I'm not so sure you will care, but it was something that I thought was interesting."

"Try me."

"Okay. Remember the lesson this afternoon with Professor Tooth?"

"Yeah. *History of the Middle Ages.*" Darrell looked a bit sheepish. "I hadn't really intended to go, but it was pretty interesting."

"I thought so, too. Anyway, remember how Professor Tooth said that people used to use art to record daily life? Then she talked about some of the paintings that showed how people lived from day to day."

Darrell nodded. "I felt like she was looking at me the whole time. Trying to tie history to a topic like art that really interested me, or something."

"I didn't notice that," Kate admitted. "But later this afternoon after my programming class with Mr. Neuron, I was walking down the hall. Professor Tooth saw me and gave me this. She mentioned how she thought you might like to see it."

Kate paused to lean against a boulder at the base of the cliff path. She pulled a small envelope out of the binder she carried and passed it to Darrell. Darrell leaned against the boulder too, and the two of them looked carefully at the picture that Darrell pulled from the envelope. It was a small print of a detailed woodcut, depicting a number of very disturbing images.

"What do you make of that?" asked Kate. "It's from a book called *Medieval Art*. She said the book showed how people lived during that period of time."

Darrell looked for several minutes at the print in silence. It was quite primitive in style and depicted people working in fields and along the streets of an old village. A closer look showed several people on the ground, in various stages of decomposition, many in the form of skeletons. Other skeletons walked through the picture, some carrying scythes, others rosaries.

Darrell looked at Kate. "This must've been done around the time of the Black Plague that swept through Europe." She thought for a moment. In the distance, they heard the bell chime for dinner.

"I think I know why she gave me this," Darrell said finally, as they started up the winding path. "Remember how Professor Tooth said that art was often more reliable than written history during those times? She said only the elite were literate, and they didn't ever look at life through the eyes of all the poor people. As we left the classroom, I mentioned to her that I never saw people who weren't physically perfect depicted in portraits." The line between her eyebrows deepened. "I guess she wanted to show me that I was wrong."

They puffed their way up to the top of the cliff path, Darrell limping slightly.

When she had caught her breath at the top, Kate changed the subject. "The other reason that I came to find you was that Mr. Neuron said that the school was having a bit of trouble with people poaching crabs on school property. He told us to watch out for any suspicious activity. I thought you should know, since you seem to like walking on the beach by yourself a lot."

Darrell laughed a little as she held open the front door. "I guess I'd better talk to Mr. Neuron, then."

As they sat down to dinner, she told Kate about the incident with the crab trappers the day before. Kate was appalled. "You need to tell Professor Tooth, Darrell. Throwing a rock like that is common assault!"

Darrell shook her head. "He would just say that I threw a rock at him first."

A boy sitting across the table from them was listening closely. He cleared his throat.

"Excuse me for interrupting," he said quietly. "But I think I've seen those guys on the beach as well. Except when I saw them, they weren't catching crabs. They were cutting up a big fish, further down the beach, past the rocky spit."

"They might have been cutting bait for their traps," said Kate, triumphantly.

Darrell looked with interest at the boy who had spoken. "I'm Darrell Connor," she said.

"Brodie Sun." He stuck out his hand, and Darrell shook it.

Kate smiled. "And now you know who 'this Brodie guy' is!"

CHAPTER FOUR

Darrell was given her first real challenge of the summer the following week when Mr. Gill assigned a self-portrait in painting class. Though she actually enjoyed portraiture as a rule, Darrell scowled into the mirror Mr. Gill had set up beside her easel. Glaring back at her was a girl with medium brown hair caught up in a ponytail, deep brown eyes, and olive skin. Looking to see that the teacher's attention was on another student, she turned the mirror aside. *Who wants to see a painting of some kid with one leg?* She spent the rest of the class in a black temper, sketching Picasso-like images made up of disjointed body parts.

Running down to the beach after class felt like a huge relief. To take her mind off the unwanted challenge of the self-portrait, Darrell focused her energy on training Delaney to do a few tricks. She talked the soft-hearted school cook into buying a large bag of dog food, and every day for that week and the next she ran down to the beach after art to play with Delaney. She crawled into his special tunnel to feed him and fill his water bowl. She sat on the sand with treats in her pocket and taught him to sit and to stay, to roll over and to lie down on command. And every day she would think up a new art project that would allow her to delay working on the self-portrait for one more day.

Over the next several nights while Kate tapped away at her computer and Lily was blissfully unaware of her own snores, Darrell lay in her bed and wondered about the crab trappers. It was clear they were up to something, though she wasn't yet sure what it could be. Her encounter with the bullies on the beach had left her feeling disturbed, but the mystery of the situation had a certain appeal. Mystery was one area, along with her art, where Darrell felt she had some expertise.

For many weeks after her accident, Darrell had lain in bed, feeling as though her heart had shattered and been removed along with her foot. Her beloved father was gone, her foot was gone, and she felt her life was too filled with sadness to look forward to another day. Darrell watched through half-open eyes as her mother, sick with worry, brought in a series of counsellors to try to support her devastated daughter.

None of the counsellors helped. Nothing helped. Until Darrell's Uncle Frank remembered his own broken leg.

Her mother's brother had been into the hospital many times over the weeks after the accident. Darrell was his only niece, and she knew how his heart bled every time he saw her small, white face on the pillow. After six long weeks of staring at the walls, Darrell looked up one afternoon to see Uncle Frank standing in the doorway with something under his arm.

He told her the story of his own broken leg, snapped through the femur when he took a header off his bike when he was twelve. He had spent three weeks in traction then, he said, and he fervently believed that a woman named Agatha Christie had saved his life.

The package under his arm was *Murder on the Orient Express*. Darrell picked it up after he left her room and in an hour she was hooked. Something in the essence of a story that revolved around the death of a man on a famous train swept her away from her own misery. In the end, she read everything that Agatha Christie had ever written, from *The Murder of Roger Ackroyd* to *Curtain*. She moved on to Dick Francis, Daphne Du Maurier, and PD James, and she never looked back. Something about the way mysteries were always solved in the books she read appealed to her sense of order.

Sometime after she turned eleven, Darrell discovered that when she concentrated on drawing, the real world would melt away and she could step into the pictures that poured out of her charcoal pencil as easily as she slipped into the lives of Jane Marple and Adam Dalgliesh. She journeyed into her creativity, preferring it to the real world. Her love of order and her ability to shape the worlds under her pencil pulled her into the stories and drawings that became a more desirable place to live than in the real world with a missing leg and a dead father.

As she rolled over to sleep, Darrell decided that it was high time she put her expertise toward solving the mystery of the crab trappers on the beach.

Darrell spent part of the following morning soaking up facts about disease and despair in the Middle Ages. Much of Professor Tooth's history class reminded her of an Ellis Peters novel, and she relished every moment.

After lunch, there was half an hour of free time before afternoon classes commenced. Darrell decided to forget about her self-portrait and instead get to the bottom of the crab trappers mystery. She wanted to head straight down to the beach to see if she could spot any signs of suspicious activity, but she was worried about going alone: if she ran into the trappers again, she'd need witnesses to verify her story if they started any trouble. Spotting Brodie and Kate near the lunchroom, she asked if they might be interested in a walk by the water. Exchanging a surprised glance, they agreed, so Darrell grabbed a notebook and the three of them set off down the winding path to the beach.

They had walked just past the small rocky spit that protruded like a pointing finger into the fjord when they heard a taunting voice call out from behind Kate and Brodie. The voice belonged to one of a group of three boys lounging on the beach behind the rocks.

"Hey, Slant!"

Kate whirled around, her face burning. "*What* did you say?"

"I wasn't talkin' to you, Red. I was talkin' to your *boyfriend*."

It was impossible for Kate's face to become any redder, so she turned purple, instead. "You … you … PIG," she spluttered. "He's not my boyfriend, he's my friend! And … *what* did you call him?" Brodie put a calm hand on her arm and smiled at her kindly. He turned to their sneering tormentor.

"Sorry, I didn't catch your name," he said quietly.

"It's Conrad Kennedy, like that's any of your business," he snickered, and his friends drew closer.

"But what's it to you ... *Slant?*" Both of Conrad's cronies laughed.

"Well ... *Conrad*," Brodie continued so quietly that the group surrounding them all leaned in closer. "My name is Broderick Stewart Sun. My friends call me Brodie. My grandmother calls me Broderick." Brodie's eyes glittered dangerously, and he straightened to his full height. "But nobody calls me Slant."

Darrell gazed with sick recognition at the boy called Conrad and cursed herself for not making a quick trip up the arbutus tree at the beginning of their walk.

Conrad got lazily to his feet and looked at the small group on the beach. He was easily three years older than any of Darrell's group, but he was short and stocky, not any taller than Brodie.

Conrad caught sight of Darrell. He sneered. "Look who's here, boys. It's Gimpy! Caught any rocks, lately, Gimpster?"

"Not lately," she snapped back. "Picked up a fishing license, yet?"

The other boys looked uncomfortable, but Conrad just smiled. He looked around.

"I don't see anyone fishing here, Gimpy. Just a group of friends enjoying the beach in the summertime." The two boys with him nodded and blatantly flexed their muscles.

"Well this happens to be a private beach, and you're trespassing." She looked at Brodie and Kate. "Let's just go back to the school, guys. We can register a complaint."

The three started to walk away. Conrad leaned in front of Darrell. "After you," he said with a sneer. As she stepped by him he stuck out his foot to trip her. She stumbled but managed to stay upright.

Kate, walking behind Darrell, deftly turned and, using Conrad's weight against him, slipped his protruding foot out from under him and flipped him to the ground. Conrad lay on the rocky surface, a stunned look on his face. His mouth worked as though he was going to say something, but no words came out.

"Watch your step, *Connie*," Kate said to him sweetly. "It's slippery on these rocks, and you wouldn't want to fall and *hurt* yourself."

Conrad's friends quickly scooped him to his feet and hustled him over onto their boat. Conrad, sand all over the back of his jacket, hissed, "I won't forget this. You three stay away from this beach. Consider yourselves warned." He turned to his friends. "Start the boat, Lastman," he snarled. The other two scrambled over to the outboard, and the engine roared into life.

As the boat pulled away, Brodie turned to look at Kate.

"How did you do that?" he asked, admiringly.

Kate smiled. "Tae kwon do. Third degree black belt."

Darrell and Brodie stared. "I thought you always had your nose glued to a computer screen," marvelled Darrell.

"A girl's got to do something when she's away from school," grinned Kate.

"Wow." Brodie shook his head and looked admiringly at Kate and Darrell. "One thing about this place; it's never boring!"

That night, Darrell was back in her bed, and Lily and Kate were in their accustomed positions, snoring and computing, respectively. She pulled out her notebook and began writing down questions about Conrad and his friends.

Who is Conrad Kennedy?
Why does he feel that he can get away with poaching?
How come he acts like he owns the beach?
Why do he and his friends react so violently when someone steps on the beach?
What are they hiding?

She thought back to earlier in the day when she had made her report to a frowning Arthur Gill. When Darrell had mentioned that Brodie had asked Conrad's name, a light went on behind Mr. Gill's eyes. "Did you say Conrad Kennedy?" he asked, slowly. "I know that boy." He dropped his chin to his chest and thought for a moment, and then looked back up at Darrell. "His father owns some land on the small island you can see out in the fjord to the south of the school's property. I believe his family are fishers."

Darrell snorted. "That may be so, but does he have the right to be running crab traps just off the beach line here? I asked him if he had a license, and he didn't. And yet he didn't seem worried about it at all. He acted like he owned the place."

Arthur Gill looked serious. "Well if he *is* crabbing along this stretch of coast without a license, he's going to have a bit of a problem." He made a few notes and promised to inform Professor Tooth of both incidents. Darrell left the office feeling somewhat relieved to have finally been able to tell the story to an adult who took her seriously.

Tapping her pencil against her notebook in bed, Darrell realized that she had nothing really solid to go on with Conrad Kennedy. She decided that she needed to come up with a plan to catch him poaching crabs red-handed. It was time for a little more observation in her trusty arbutus tree.

For the next few days, Darrell spent much of her free time sitting in the arbutus and watching the beach, occasionally making notes or sketching in her book. Invariably, Delaney was curled up nearby.

She noticed that Kate and Brodie seemed to have decided to keep their distance for a while. One sunny afternoon while perched in her tree, Darrell saw them sitting together on a log in the garden, watching Lily training in the water while they ate their lunch. Their voices carried on the salty air, and Darrell pretended she couldn't hear their conversation.

"That girl is quite a swimmer," remarked Brodie admiringly as Lily stroked by, her brown arms glistening in the sun.

Kate rolled her eyes. "You should hear her talk! If that were an Olympic event, she'd win gold for sure." She took a bite of her sandwich. "Come to think of it, she'd do pretty well in the snoring Olympics as well."

"She probably needs her sleep, after all these hard workouts," Brodie said, sensibly. He shaded his eyes and looked up toward the arbutus tree. Darrell bent her head to her notebook.

"Why is she still in that tree?" asked Kate.

"I don't know." He looked back down at Lily, not meeting Kate's eyes. "I feel kind of sorry for her," he admitted.

Kate looked quizzical. "For Lily?"

Brodie laughed. "Not Lily. Darrell."

Kate shrugged. "I do too, sometimes. But every time I try to talk to her, she's either rude or nasty." She glanced up at the tree to see Darrell scribbling away in her book. "I've known her for a long time, you know."

"Have you?" Brodie looked embarrassed. "Ah ... how did it happen?"

"Her leg, you mean?"

"Yeah."

Kate sighed. "It was a really sad story. She was in a motorcycle accident with her dad. He died and she lost her foot."

Brodie winced. "She probably needs to talk about it to get the bitterness out of her system."

Kate laughed, and looked with interest at Brodie. "That doesn't sound like something most boys would say."

Brodie looked a bit defensive. "Let's just say I've had a few of my own problems. I think talking them out helps a bit, that's all."

Kate looked out at Lily, still swimming like a fish in the ocean. She bit her lip.

"Do you mean problems like with what Conrad said the other day?"

Brodie stiffened. "What do you mean?"

"When he called you Slant. I mean, that's really racist. I couldn't believe he could say something like that."

Brodie shrugged. "He called Darrell a gimp, too. He was full of kind thoughts." Brodie looked serious for a moment, then brightened. "Loved that little flip that you pulled on him, though. That kind of made up for the name-calling."

Kate smiled. "Glad you liked it."

They stood up to head back to the school. Darrell slipped down out of her tree and followed.

Brodie spoke again. "You know, sometimes I know how Darrell feels. My dad's family came to Canada to help build the railroad in 1887. They were from Shanghai. That was five generations ago." Kate nodded as Brodie continued. "My mother is actually from Scotland, but she moved here to go to university, and that's where she met and married my dad." He thought for a moment. "Growing up on the West Coast has been great. There are people of all backgrounds here and almost everybody is pretty cool. Most people I have met are a little more enlightened than those idiots on the beach." He reddened, slightly. "It just gets to me when people judge others purely on how they look. They did it to Darrell and they did it to me. I guess I shouldn't let it get to me."

Kate nodded. "You're right, they were just idiots," she said.

Brodie looked serious. "Still … I have run into a fair share of racists in my time. It feels awful when some jerk tries to make you feel like you don't fit in for a reason as lame as the colour of your skin or the shape of your eyes."

Kate looked horrified. "You don't get that feeling here at Eagle Glen, do you?"

Brodie smiled as they rounded the corner to the school. "Our beach idiots excepted, not really. But I think I know someone else who feels like an outsider." Darrell froze, and leaned up against the corner, straining to hear.

"I think I will try again, to see if she'll talk about it," Brodie said firmly.

Kate laughed. "Good luck! If she gets too hard to handle, just call on me. I think I know a few tae kwon do moves that will hold her in place so you can you get away safely!"

Darrell silently steamed as the voices faded into the school doorway. She bit her lip and then, after a few moments, trailed into the school.

At dinner that night, Professor Tooth stood up with archaeology teacher Mr. Dickerman to announce that Brodie Sun had won the Katzenberg Award for an essay he had written about ancient arrow heads found on the west coast of Canada. With the award came a scholarship that would offset the cost of his summer school courses at Eagle Glen. Everyone applauded politely.

After dinner, Brodie asked Darrell if she would be interested in looking at some rock formations on the beach. She thought about refusing and then swallowed her pride and agreed. They walked down to the beach and followed the rock face for some distance. Delaney met them on the sand and trailed them down to the rocks. Brodie pointed out several fossils embedded in the cliff walls. After half an hour or so of hard fossil hunting, they headed for a log in the sand near the cliff face.

Darrell sat down on the log and ran her toes through the sand. Delaney curled up on the sand between them. The late evening sun felt warm on her face, and she turned to Brodie.

"Your family must be proud of you," she said quietly. "About the award, I mean."

"Yeah, I guess so," he answered.

There was a long silence. Brodie looked down and collected his nerve as he glanced at Darrell's leg. "How did you lose your foot?" he asked quietly, his face carefully blank.

Darrell felt her anger from earlier in the day surge. "How did you get to be such an idiot?" she replied with a snarl. "It just happened, that's all. A long time ago." She fell silent, and then looked at him defiantly. "I don't have to tell you anything, y'know. It's none of your business."

Brodie looked embarrassed. "You're right," he said, standing up. "You don't have to tell me anything." Darrell lifted her head, and Brodie looked straight into her eyes. "I'm sorry. I just wanted to learn more about you. We'll be in school together all summer and ..." he paused. "I just thought you might *want* to tell me."

"It's okay," Darrell cut him off, her anger breaking. She ducked her head again, and picked up a stick from the sand. "I'm just a little sensitive about it. My foot was amputated after I broke it really badly in an accident three years ago." She sighed. "It's a long story."

Brodie winced and looked again at Darrell. She could feel the wind blow her hair around lightly, and tried to blink away the tears in her eyes. He bent to pick up a rock and tossed it out toward the surf.

Darrell tapped the toes of her prosthetic foot with a stick and remembered the day when, at ten years of age, her life had changed forever. She lost her father and her leg in one terrible instant.

Darrell threw the stick violently at the sea. She opened her mouth to say something sharp, closed it again, and burst into tears. She cried bitterly for a few minutes. As her sobs tapered off, Brodie handed her an old paper napkin.

"Sorry," he said. "It is clean, it's just been in my pocket for a while."

Darrell sniffed and wiped her eyes.

"It's okay," she said indistinctly, and a moment later she remembered to say, "Thanks." Brodie sat back down. Darrell began to speak as though in a dream, slowly at first and then with increasing speed.

"I can hardly remember it," she began. "I never really lived with my dad. He and my mother split up when I was really young. He worked as an extra in the movie industry and just drove around from job to job. He would rent a place to live for a few months and then just move on." She blew her nose and continued. "My mom says it was no life for someone who had a kid, but he just kept doing it."

"How was your dad involved in the accident?" Brodie asked.

Darrell took a deep breath and told Brodie the story. She spoke about the day in the summer when she was ten, driving down a winding highway on their way home to Vancouver after an afternoon of swimming and ice cream. Their motorcycle was blind-sided by a car, and she and her father had been thrown in front of a truck by the force of the crash. In his final millisecond, he put the strength of all his love into a brutal push that sent Darrell spinning sideways out of the path of the oncoming vehicle that took his life. She flew through the air with sickening speed and landed on her feet, improbably upright, at the side of the road. Her left foot was driven eight inches into the soft dirt that edged the highway.

Her right foot landed squarely on the asphalt at thirty-five kilometres an hour. Her ankle, broken once when she was six, shattered a second time, more permanently. The pain had been so pure, clear, and exquisite that Darrell, mercifully, had fainted immediately.

In the hours after the accident, the doctors (not including Darrell's mother, who found herself to be more shattered than Darrell's ankle) worked long and hard to try to save the foot. They thought about re-building the ankle, replacing the joint, microsurgery, and more. But Darrell's ankle, in spite of the indomitable spirit of its owner, refused to participate in the healing process. Infection set in and a further surgery was performed, removing the shattered bone, skin, sinew, and flesh below the knee. Pain, physiotherapy, and prosthesis — the three terrible P's — had followed.

Brodie looked horrified. "It's amazing you're alive!"

Darrell nodded. "It is, I guess. I never really thought of it that way. I lost my dad and my leg — well, part of it anyway — and for a long time I felt like I had lost my life, too. Things just aren't the same anymore."

Brodie put his head into his hands, and they sat in silence for a few moments.

"I'm really sorry," he said quietly. "Does your leg still hurt?"

Darrell smiled. "Just my ankle," she said ruefully. "It really kills me on rainy nights."

Brodie looked baffled. He looked more closely at the prosthetic leg. "Your ankle?" he said slowly. "But, you lost your leg below the knee."

Darrell shrugged and tucked her hair behind her ear. "Tell that to my ankle," she said. "I can always tell when the rain is coming."

A buzzer sounded in the distance. Darrell and Brodie looked up. They could see Kate running across the sand, waving.

"I guess it's time to go back," said Brodie.

Darrell jumped up. "Come on, I'll race you!" She took off like a bullet in the characteristic hop-skip running style that was all her own. Caught by surprise, it took Brodie a minute to realize what was happening. He was about to be creamed by a girl with one leg.

He scooped up his pack and ran after Darrell. "Wait up!" he called without thinking. He and Darrell reached Kate together, Delaney right at their heels. Gasping for breath, they looked at each other and burst out laughing at Kate's shocked expression. They turned and headed up the winding path toward the school.

CHAPTER FIVE

Since the accident, Darrell had never cried in public. Much like her daily sessions standing on cold concrete, not crying was a point of pride, a way to prove something to herself. She was surprised that the talk with Brodie and even breaking down and crying did not make her feel angry at her own weakness. Instead, for some reason, things felt better. Their short walk left Darrell feeling lighter in spirit than she had for a long time. Things had also improved with Kate. Darrell still wasn't sure she was ready to trust anyone, but she might try to discuss her lingering questions about the crab trappers, if she could manage to do it without alienating Kate and Brodie again.

Darrell tried to draw on these positive feelings, and she approached her self-portrait with a new vigour. In the weeks since Mr. Gill had given the assignment, she had struggled to find a direction to take. Every class, she had walked from easel to easel, looking at the choices the other students had made. One portrait took on the formal tones of a Rembrandt while the next had a distinct Andy Warhol feel.

The morning after the walk with Brodie, Darrell stood at her easel and clutched her paintbrush with the familiar feeling of anger and puzzlement gnawing at her. She glanced up at Mr. Gill as he helped out a student across the room. Once again, the face of Leonardo da Vinci flashed through her mind. In less than a moment, she made a decision.

At least Mr. Gill doesn't dictate one style over the other, she thought as she dug around in her box of supplies. *Let's see what he thinks of this.*

At last, she had begun her self-portrait.

When she woke early the following Saturday and glanced at her watch, the date caught her eye. Darrell realized with surprise that she had been at Eagle Glen for nearly a month. It was not yet six o'clock, so she pulled the pillow over her head to try to go back to sleep. Eagle Glen catered only to boarding students, so classes were not completely cancelled on the weekends but instead ran to a modified schedule, allowing more free time for personal interests. Darrell planned to spend the day mucking about with her self-portrait in the art studio. She was working with acrylics for the first time and really enjoying the flexibility of the colour and texture of the paint.

Lying in bed, her mind still whirled with the questions she had written in her notebook. She found that she could not go back to sleep after all. Breakfast wasn't served until nine on Saturdays. Darrell grabbed her sandals and her backpack with her camera and art supplies and ran down to the kitchen anyway. She poured a cup of coffee and quickly headed outside to size up the day. The sun had not yet risen over the mountains, and Darrell walked over to the concrete slab outside the kitchen door and automatically stepped up on it in her bare feet to drink her coffee.

She thought about the time she had spent every day, training Delaney, and how she had just taught him how to sniff out which of two closed hands held a treat. She was particularly proud of the way he seriously placed his paw on the hand holding the treat and then waited patiently for his reward. Delaney was a swift learner, and she had a sudden urge to see him before class.

Maybe I'll skip this today, she thought suddenly and hopped off the slab, before her bare foot had even a chance to feel cold. She drained her coffee, put on her sandals, and then ran over and scrambled up the arbutus. She had not noticed Conrad on the beach since the incident with Kate and Brodie, though she had spied him racing in his boat with his friends. He had been speeding along the north end of the beach near a group of large boulders that had tumbled from the cliffs down into the sea.

From her perch the beach looked deserted, and she decided to go down and investigate something she had seen on her walk with Brodie. She felt in her pocket for the bun and bacon she had taken from the kitchen on the way to grab her coffee.

The boulders near where she had seen Conrad in his boat formed a barrier that effectively hid part of the rock wall from anyone further down the beach and created a little protected cove. Darrell walked down to have a look at the cove and also at a little cleft she had noticed in the rock while hunting for fossils with Brodie.

As Darrell emerged from the winding path, Delaney bounded joyfully up the beach to meet her. He snuffled her hand, and she gave him the bacon and bun she had brought from the kitchen.

"We'll check your water later, Delaney," she said. "Let's go see if Conrad's been on this part of the beach." Glancing around a little nervously, she made sure that there were no boats in the water or distant figures on the stretch of shoreline before she headed back toward the rock wall.

The morning was still grey and the water was calm, but the humid, sluggish air warned of an approaching storm. The high tide meant Darrell and Delaney had to skirt very close to the cliffs to get around the massive reach of boulders. Looking above the tide line on the sand, Darrell noticed many footprints criss-crossing each other, blurry and indistinct in the grey light of early morning.

She bent down to study them more closely when Delaney gave a short bark. Darrell looked over to see he was pawing at a small white plastic container, about the size and shape of a shoebox, that had fallen over onto the sand. She ran over to find a whole stack of similar boxes crammed in between two of the large boulders. If the top box had not fallen out of its place, Darrell would have never noticed them, as they were covered with camouflage netting and were almost completely hidden from view.

Darrell looked into the box that was tipped over on the beach. It was filled with dozens of compact disc cases and a sealed bag of what looked like computer components. She sat back on her heels and thought for a moment.

"There's something going on here that's bigger than crab poaching, Delaney," she said thoughtfully. Looking again to see that no one was around, she turned back and stepped slowly along the face of the rock wall. Near the tide line, where the water lapped the shore, Darrell found what she was looking for. The cleft in the rock wall was very narrow, and Darrell reached her arm inside to see if there would be room to slide into it. To her surprise, she felt nothing with her arm except open air. She squeezed around the corner and found that the cleft opened up into a cave. It was not very bright, lit only through a crack in the rock face above.

Darrell peered out the entrance of the cave and discovered that she had a perfect view of the little protected cove and the stash of boxes on the beach. She looked delightedly at the dog.

"This is it, Delaney! This is our way of catching Connie at whatever he's up to." She ruffled the dog's fur and then gave him the signal for *Stay* she had been practicing with him over the past few weeks. Delaney dropped to the sand and wriggled contentedly, his head in his paws. He looked up at her, raising alternating eyebrows.

She dropped to her knees in the sand and opened her backpack. Inside, among her art supplies, she found the small camera that she used for taking landscape pictures. She also grabbed a small flashlight. It was dark and dank in the cave, and she wasn't sure she wanted to know if anything lived inside.

As Darrell slipped her camera and flashlight into her pocket she noticed the medieval woodcut print tucked in the side of her pack. She slid it into her pocket to look at later and ran up the beach to find a fallen branch on the sand. Walking quickly backwards down the beach with the branch dragging behind her, she carefully obliterated her footprints.

She poked her head around the corner of the cave, and Delaney sat up in his spot.

"Good dog, Delaney!" Darrell fed him some of the dry dog food in her pack as a reward for his long stay. She dropped the cedar branch behind her on the sandy floor of the cave. In the distance she heard the roar of a motor. She checked her watch: 6:20 A.M.

Silently she readjusted her position, carefully stretching each leg before returning to her spot in the sand. Her biggest worry right now was the light. "Next time, I'll have to bring Kate," she muttered under her breath. Darrell's camera was the simple single-action, point-and-shoot variety. Kate had a great digital camera with some kind of special ability to take pictures in near-darkness. Her expertise with digital photography would have been helpful, though Darrell was doubtful of Kate's ability to rise this early. She clicked off the flash button and leaned against the clammy rock face inside the cave. The air felt dank and still.

Delaney lay quietly on the sand. His wet nose touched her ankle, and she bent to give him a reassuring pat. She looked into his brown eyes and felt happy for his company.

A gentle beam of light slid through the darkness of the cave. Darrell silently gave thanks. The sun had not yet risen over the mountains, but the sky had lightened and daylight slipped through the crack in the rock face above. With daylight came a better chance to get pictures. At the same time, her heart sank. Daylight also meant a greater chance of being caught herself, a prospect she didn't relish. She remembered with a pang that she had not told anyone where she was going.

Her chest rose and fell silently. She could feel her heart pounding in her ears. It sounded much louder to her than the waves lapping on the beach.

All her energy was poured into listening.

The engine noise died in the distance, so at first she wasn't sure. The sound, a low crunch, sounded like a part of the background: the noise of the tide gliding in over the rocks, broken shells, and sand on the beach. She heard it again and knew it for what it was. A footstep. Darrell tightened her grip on the camera, drew her breath in through her teeth, and waited. Everything depended on her silence right now.

The voices grew louder, though whoever was out there was speaking in low tones and was still at some distance from Darrell's hiding place in the cave. Delaney stirred, his ears forward and his eyes alert. Darrell gave him the hand signal for *Stay*, and he remained motionless in his spot on the sand. She slid silently closer to the cave entrance, her camera poised.

Darrell peeked with one eye around the edge of the rock that guarded the entrance to the cave. Lichen scraped her cheek, but she ignored it as she aimed her camera at the action unfolding nearby.

A small boat was pulled up past the water line on the beach inside the tiny cove formed by the sweep of boulders that marched from the cliffs to the shore. The spot was completely shielded from the view of the school by the giant rocks. Two figures were loading the white plastic boxes into the boat, and Darrell could see that one of them was Conrad, dressed from head to toe in black. He wore a black woollen hat on his head and had smudges of mud smeared on his face. She pulled her head back into the cave for a moment, stifling a smile. He was clearly taking this commando business seriously.

Checking her camera, Darrell could see she had several shots left. She took a step backwards to make sure that no one outside would hear the advancing of the film, and her foot jammed against something soft. Delaney gave a little squeak as Darrell tumbled to the sandy floor of the cave with a thud.

Darrell could hear a sudden silence as all activity outside came to an abrupt halt.

"Did you hear anything?" she heard Conrad hiss anxiously on the beach. She sat on the floor of the cave, frozen with fear, her leg wrapped around Delaney's front paws, over which she had tripped. She didn't dare to move for fear of further alerting Conrad, but she had fallen in a position where she could not see what was going on outside.

Another voice, low pitched and rough, spoke out.

"It may have just been the sound of the water in the rocks," the voice began. "Or it could be a problem. Conrad! You told me there wouldn't be any problems."

Darrell could hear Conrad again. She hardly recognized his voice. She realized that he sounded scared. She had never heard him sound like *that* before!

"It's okay, Dad. I'm sure it was just the tide. This place is just fine, believe me. I've been casing it out for months. This stretch of beach is deserted. None of the brainoid kids who go to that school ever come down here." His voice gained more confidence. "No problem, Dad. This place is really safe."

The low-pitched, rough voice came again. "I hope you're right, kid. Because the risks are all yours. You're the one with everything to lose." Darrell could hear the gravel crunch. "We're already more than an hour behind schedule because you couldn't get out of bed this morning. So, get moving!" the voice barked, and the sounds of large objects being slid along the surface of the beach began again.

Darrell reached for her camera, and then closed her eyes in despair. The cave floor was completely dry, but her fall had sprung the back of the camera open. The film, exposed, lay curled inside the camera like a dead snake.

Anger flooded through Darrell, and her face grew red as she thought of the opportunity she had lost. She struggled to stand and pressed her face around the corner again. One glimpse had her quickly diving for cover. The men were less than ten metres from her hiding place in the cave. The pile of plastic containers had shrunk, with most of them stacked in the boat.

Darrell could feel her panic rising. If the smugglers searched the rocks for a spot to hide more containers, they would surely find her cave. It was difficult to find, but a thorough search would doubtless bring it to light as an ideal hiding place. Darrell picked up the camera and quietly whispered *Come* to Delaney. He got up, tail swaying gently, and padded over to her side. She grabbed the tree branch and hastily tried to obliterate as many footprints on the floor of the cave as she could see in the dim light.

Walking backwards, Darrell moved past the point at the back of the cave where the walls narrowed and the ceiling dropped down. She tried to stop and catch her breath, but sheer panic drove her further back and down as she sought out a place where Conrad and his father would not immediately find her. She patted the small flashlight in her pocket and then tucked her backpack behind a small rock on the sand.

Peering into the darkness, she turned around and tried to make out any detail of her surroundings. The cave was pitch black and smelled of salt and seaweed. In spite of her fear of something lurking in its musty recesses Darrell did not want to risk turning on the flashlight. She dropped the branch near the pack and, running her hands along the wall, continued to creep her way back into the cave.

The floor began to level out. Although she was moving slowly, after about five minutes, she began to feel safer. The men would want to leave quickly with their boat before anyone noticed them on the shore. Darrell stopped for a moment to reach down. Delaney was right at her side, his warm breath reassuring on her hand.

After a short rest, she continued to move deeper into the cave, using her hands to feel her way along the walls. "Another ten metres," she whispered, "and we'll turn the light on, okay Delaney?"

Her fingers felt raw from rubbing the uneven rock along the cave wall. Still, she hadn't bumped her head or fallen over again, and that was something. She continued with her slow crab-walk, sideways and downward. Darrell had just decided to turn on her flashlight when Delaney began to whine.

She stopped, keeping one hand on the wall for balance, and put her other hand down onto his head, trying to reassure him with her touch. "Shhh, Delaney," she whispered, "it's okay ..." Suddenly, a searing pain shot through her hand and down her arm. It felt like she was receiving an electric shock from the cave wall, but she was unable to move her hand. She instinctively clutched Delaney's collar, and the cave began to whirl about her, making her head spin.

The pain was sickening, and Darrell closed her eyes and moaned.

She found herself curled up in a ball on the sand and rolled on the ground, writhing with nausea. She felt like she had just been punched in the stomach, and she fought for breath. Moving made her feel worse so she lay very still, feeling the nausea ebb away like the pull of the tide. Her head ached, and it was several minutes before she felt able to sit up. She opened her eyes to a dull glow that illuminated the area around her. Looking up, she could see a symbol on the wall of the cave above where she lay curled on the sand. It appeared to be lit from within, and it cast a dim light on the walls of the deep inner cave.

Forgetting her headache, Darrell slowly stood up. She wanted to take a closer look. The symbol on the wall appeared to be illuminated through the rock. It took the shape of a deciduous tree and was about six inches high. As Darrell watched, the light gradually faded away, as if withdrawing back into the rock itself. In a matter of moments, Darrell once again found herself in total darkness.

The pain that had shot through her arm was gone, but her fingers felt numb and limp. She rubbed her hands together and sank back down to the ground.

"I must have cracked my elbow against the rock, eh Delaney?" Darrell began, and then realized that she could not hear Delaney panting, or feel him anywhere beside her. Panic slid back into her stomach, and she spent several frantic minutes feeling around in the sand of the cave floor, trying to find the dog.

After smacking her face twice into the rocks, the second time bashing her lower lip into her teeth and cutting it, Darrell managed to get hold of herself. She sat back down on the sandy floor and took several deep breaths.

"Delaney," she called softly, "Delaney, come."

No answer.

Darrell called again several times, but she realized with despair that the dog was missing. With her thoughts still fuzzy and Delaney gone, it made it hard to decide what to do next.

"One thing is certain," she whispered to herself. "If I don't find Delaney before Conrad does, he'll know

I'm here. I've got to find that dog." She licked the sore spot on her lip and got to her hands and knees.

Scared to touch the wall of the cave that had given her such a shock, she decided to crawl, using the sand and the rising level of the ground to help find her way out. It was slower than walking, but she made steady progress as the sandy surface slanted upwards. Her prosthetic leg felt heavy and she still felt quite tired and not herself. As she crawled, her nausea lessened and she found herself more able to think.

"It must have been some kind of electric shock," she thought. "A charge or something that came through the rock. I don't think the rock was wet ... if it was, it probably would have been much worse." She paused, panting from the effort of dragging her leg up the sandy slope in the dark, and without thinking leaned back against the cave wall.

As she felt the rock at her back, Darrell started, but nothing happened. No shock, no flash of light, no glowing symbols ... just the solid rock of the cave wall. Darrell reached her hand up to touch the rock when she realized that she could see. Gradually, the level of light had been growing as she made her way closer to the mouth of the cave. In spite of her fear of running into Conrad, she almost laughed with relief.

Darrell decided that the light had increased enough to walk. It was still very dim in the cave, but she could see enough to make her way slowly upwards. As she reached the place where the ground began to flatten out, in the distance ahead she could just make out the entrance.

She paused to make sure that no one had entered since she had fled into the cave earlier. There were no footprints or signs of anything different, but she walked cautiously, no longer talking to herself but instead listening carefully for sounds of Conrad and his father. Creeping forward, she noticed a large brownish rock by the very entrance of the cave. Looking closely in the dim light, she realized that it wasn't a rock.

"Delaney!" she cried aloud, caution forgotten. She ran over to the dog and dropped down on her knees beside him. For one quick moment her heart leapt into her throat, as he was curled up so peacefully she thought he must be dead. At her touch he raised his head and, sleepy-eyed, thumped his tail on the ground in greeting.

She plunged her face into the fur of his side, delighted and relieved to find him at last. After a quiet reunion, Darrell lifted her head to listen for any noise outside the cave, but could only hear the sound of the surf on the shore. She risked another whisper.

"Where's your collar, boy?" Delaney just thumped his tail and rested his paw on Darrell's leg. "I grabbed your collar just as the shock hit," she said slowly, remembering. "You must have slipped out of it, and I guess I dropped it in the dark." She looked at him sternly. "Why did you run away, Delaney? I need you to stay right beside me." The dog thumped his tail again. Darrell stood and peeked out.

"Looks like the coast is clear. Come on, Delaney. Let's see what Conrad has left for us to sniff out."

CHAPTER SIX

Her aching arm and head and the resulting nausea in the cave were nothing compared to the series of shocks Darrell received as she stepped out into the open. Delaney led the way, bouncing out into the sunlight joyfully. Darrell took a step forward, and then stopped. Her leg felt heavy, and she knew something was wrong, but her eyes were drawn in amazement toward Delaney. The dog spun around, waiting for Darrell to follow, tail wagging. His energy and the light from his eyes were unmistakable.

"Your coat," whispered Darrell, and she sank to the ground in surprise. "What's happened to you, boy?" For something certainly had happened to Delaney since he had slipped into the cave with Darrell only a short while before. His coat had been golden, long and gorgeous. His gently waving tail had begun as deep gold and faded to white at the end of its long feathers. However, the dog in front of Darrell now bore no resemblance to the Delaney who had been with her moments before.

His coat was brown and curly. He was clipped unevenly and one side of his fur was singed back, almost to the skin. His ears slid forward in a most un-Delaney-like way. He was smaller and looked terribly thin. And yet Darrell knew, looking into his eyes, that this was Delaney. She swallowed.

"Delaney, sit!" she commanded, her voice hoarse with shock. The dog sat, tail wagging.

She swept her arm down in the special signal she had taught Delaney, indicating that he should lie down and stay. The dog dropped to the ground like a shot and looked up at her, raising alternating eyebrows.

"Good boy, Delaney," Darrell whispered. He wagged his tail and wiggled nearer. Darrell closed her eyes and rubbed them with her fingers, and then looked at Delaney again. He looked back at her, eyes warm and brown. Darrell rolled on to one knee and prepared to stand up when she received her second jolt in under a minute. This one knocked her back down onto the ground, her heart pounding. She looked down and saw that she was no longer wearing jeans. Instead, she was wearing a long skirt of thick brown wool. At the hem of the skirt, her left foot protruded, encased in a worn brown leather boot, soled in wood and caked with a combination of mud and sand. Where her right foot should be was a splintered stub of wood, like the end of a crutch.

Darrell let out a choking sob. Her head began to swim. She put her face in her hands and closed her eyes tightly, then as quickly opened them again. Everything looked the same. She reached down and pulled the hem of the dress up slowly to see the stump of her right leg tightly bound to a wooden splint, ending in a peg leg like a pirate would wear. No plastic foot. No prosthesis at all, really. Just a wooden peg, bound tightly to the base of her leg.

Looking around, Darrell became aware that more than just she and Delaney had changed. As she lifted her head and gazed about for the first time, she realized that she was sitting on a beach against a rocky outcropping, looking up at the walls of what looked like a very dirty and ancient town. Along the shore the rotting hulls of many wooden boats lay like the corpses of sea creatures, thrusting their broken ribs toward the sky. She swallowed again and struggled to her feet.

Delaney barked and ran up the rocky beach, so unlike the one she had been standing on when she entered the cave. Unsure of what else to do and feeling dazed and sick, Darrell followed the dog who no longer looked like Delaney up some stone steps and in through the walls of the ancient town.

The sun was shining, but as Darrell crept in past the crumbling walls of the town, the small houses crowded into the shadowy lanes looked dark and grimy. She gazed around at the strange sights that met her eyes. From the boats on the beach, she determined that the main occupation of the village must be fishing.

Darrell was convinced she must be in the middle of some sort of dream or hallucination. She continued to follow the dog, who bounded along joyfully in front of her. She found balancing on the wooden peg very difficult and concentrated on making her way along the cobbled lane without falling. The ground was wet and slippery, as though from a recent rain, and yet the air was anything but fresh.

I can't be dreaming, she thought, *because dreams don't smell this terrible.* As she walked, she realized a deep gutter on one side of the lane was running with sewage. She quickly averted her eyes from the sight and held her hand up to her nose to try to block some of the smell.

"A charaid! Thalla, a chù!"

Darrell's head snapped up at the sound of the voice. Delaney barked joyfully and pranced over to a boy who looked to be about Darrell's own age. He had dropped to his knees to pat the dog and repeated his words. "Good dog! A good friend ye are."

The boy gazed up at Darrell and then, glancing around furtively, gestured for her to come nearer. Not knowing what else to do, Darrell limped toward the boy. He stood at the entrance to a small house, little more than a hovel, and yet he swung open the door as gallantly if it were the door to a castle.

"*Fàilt. Thallaibh stigh.* Come in. Welcome." He gestured to a chair inside, near a small fireplace. Darrell sat down gratefully.

"Welcome to where?" she said weakly. She had so many questions that her mind reeled. She finally settled on the most important, for the moment.

"How do you know my dog?"

The boy reached in front of Darrell and withdrew a metal ladle from the black kettle that hung from the hearth. He poured something from the ladle into a rough clay cup and pushed it into her hands.

"Ye must have many questions. Stop, and drink first." Darrell looked doubtfully at the liquid in the cup. It steamed gently.

"Tea," he said to her unasked question. "Drink it up." She took a sip obediently. It didn't have much flavour, but it was warm and gave her something to do with her hands.

Darrell was so stunned by the developments of the last fifteen minutes that she didn't even know where to begin. She started to ask again about Delaney when she realized with a shock that she was speaking the same strange words that this stranger was using. She stopped abruptly in the middle of the sentence and raised her hand to her lips in surprise.

"What language are we speaking?" she asked in a whisper.

The boy smiled. "*Gaidhlig*," he said, proudly. He swept his arm to take in the small, dark room, the floor covered in rushes. "Welcome to my home."

Children are resilient. The whole time that Darrell had been in the hospital, fighting the infection that ultimately took her foot, she heard people reassuring her mother with that phrase. *Children bounce back easily. They're so adaptable. She'll be fine, you'll see.* Darrell used to lie in the hospital bed and later in her bed at home and hear people repeating the same inane phrases. Lost her father? *She'll get over it.* Lost her foot? *She'll bounce back.* It filled her with anger, because she knew all she wanted in the world was to get her father back and to have two whole legs again.

Now, as she sat in a place where she was totally lost, where there was no explanation for why things were the way they were, where nothing could be what it seemed, she came to a bittersweet conclusion. All the hated people who had spoken to her mother during her long convalescence were right. Darrell *had* survived a terrible accident. She *had* adapted to the loss of her leg. She *had* lived through the loss of her father. Nothing she faced in this strange place could be harder than what she had already been through.

She lifted her head and stared with dry eyes at the boy, the dog, and the strange surroundings.

"*Deagh diu*," she said to the boy. "Good day. Where do we begin?"

"Please allow me to introduce myself," the boy said, formally. "My name is Luke Iainson." He inclined his head. "And I know ye be Dara, a friend to my aunt."

Darrell swallowed her nerves and nodded her head. "My name is Darrell Connor, but Dara will do just fine," she said. "How much do you know about me?"

Luke looked nervous. "My mother's sister was from Arisaig, a small village near here." At Darrell's puzzled look, he continued. "She was known to have the sight. Before the tragedy struck our village, she told me about ye." He sighed and rubbed his forehead wearily.

Darrell noticed for the first time how dirty he was. His hair, long and pulled back behind his head with a grimy piece of leather lacing, looked like it hadn't been washed or brushed for a long time. His eyes were startlingly blue, but they looked very tired. He glanced up at Darrell. His voice was quiet, remembering.

"Y'have not heard of Arisaig?" When Darrell shook her head, Luke continued, his voice dream-like. "My aunt had some … friends there. They would meet at night under the shade of an enormous rowan tree. Some

say ... some say the tree has special powers. And if anyone knew of those powers, it was my Auntie Aileen.

"One day in the summer of last year, I walked to
Arisaig, pulling our family's cart loaded with dried fish.
My family trades some of the herring from my father's
catch for a fat cow from my uncle's stock. In this way,
we can have milk and cheese and they can have fish in
the winter.

"The cart was heavy, but I didn't care, because it
was a rare day, sunny and hot, and I had time off from
polishing armour and cleaning stables.

"I walked through the centre of town. My hands
were sore — the wooden handles of the cart are splintered and old — and my throat was as dry as an old
bone. I heard a voice, calling my name...

"'Luke! *Mo cridhe*. Come to me, my heart!'

"I looked up and saw Aileen, my aunt. She stood
under the rowan tree, beckoning to me. I turned the
cart around and pulled it over to rest under the shade
of the tree. I remember the shade was wonderful, cool.
Even though there had been no breeze, I felt refreshed
under the leaves. The tree is enormous, and its branches are so thick and plentiful with leaves that its shade is
as dark as night itself.

"'Ye look so thirsty, *a mhàigein*! Stop and have a
drink.' My aunt had a skin bag of cider that she carried
on a cord on her back. She handed me the bag, and I

drank the cider. It was warm, but I was so thirsty it tasted like wine. Before I knew it, I had finished every drop.

"'I'm sorry Aileen …'

"'Don't say a word. Ye were thirsty.' She looked at my dusty clothes and boots and patted the ground near the massive trunk.

"'Sit with me a while … have a rest.'

"We sat in the shade quietly, watching the people of the village going about their business. That was a wonderful thing about my aunt. She didn't want me to talk all the time … it was fine to be silent. I picked up a berry that had fallen from the tree. It was early summer, so the berry was green, but it had the strangest shape on the end, like a five-pointed star … a pentagram.

"'Keep that,' my aunt said.

"'Why would I want a green rowan berry?'

"'It will bring ye luck, *a mhàigein*, my lovely little boy.'

"'Aileen, I am almost a grown man. Please stop calling me that.'

"She laughed and tucked her hair behind her ear. Her hair was very dark, like yers, but curly and much longer. My aunt was very beautiful. She was my mother's youngest sister, about ten years older than me, and was mother to three children of her own. It wasn't right that she called me a baby, she was really not much older than I was, anyway. I changed the subject.

"'Why are ye here, under the tree, and not at home with my cousins?'

"'They are resting through the hot part of the day, the way any sensible person is.'

"Her voice was still teasing, but at least she had stopped calling me *a mhàigein*.

"'But why *here*?'

"'I am here to gather these green berries to dry … and to meet with ye, boy.'

"This made me even more curious. The rowan berries held much value, but I did not know why. I knew some of the women of Arisaig would sell the berries along with crosses made from rowan twigs as talismans and amulets, for good luck and bad. My aunt rested her cheek against the trunk and closed her eyes. When she opened them, I could see she was no longer in the mood to tease.

"'Luke, this is a sacred place. When I heard ye were coming today, I knew I had to watch for ye … to meet ye here. There is much I have to tell. Much and little.'

"She paused and took my hand. This was unlike my sunny aunt to sound so serious. I tried to make a joke. 'Auntie Aileen, it is too hot to be so grim. The herring in my cart will dry up in the sun. Let us go back to yer home, and I will fill up this bag with more cider and put the fish in yer cellar where they will stay cool.'

"Her hand squeezed mine, and I felt that she was looking right into my soul. Her breath caught in her throat.

"'Luke, the tree has whispered to me. A terrible time is coming. There will be much death, and the loss to all will be more than ye can know.'

"I was caught up in her words. 'Aileen, how can ye know these things? And why … why do ye tell them to me?'

"'Because there is still time for ye, *mo cridhe*, and time for yer ma and sister.'

"'Now I know ye make fun of me, Auntie Aileen. Ye know I have no sister.'

"'Never mind that now, lad. The time is short, and my husband will soon awake from his sleep and need food before he goes back to work in the fields.' Her eyes travelled across the town square to rest on the dark doorway of her small cottage in the distance.

"Her face became very still, and she clutched my hand still tighter. 'Luke, I may not be able to help ye for much longer. Some evil is growing in this place, and I fear it may come to rest upon me. I trust in God for my own soul, Luke, no matter what anyone tells ye.' I started to speak, but she held up her hand. 'If I cannot help, if I am lost to ye, watch for a girl. Her name is Dara. Ye'll know her, for she will come to ye with my dog, and she will have the means to help our family through the terrible time that comes and save us from grief.'

"I pulled my hand out of hers and got to my feet. The hair on my arms was standing straight up, and I felt very strange.

"'What do ye mean, the terrible time...?' but my question was interrupted by a shout.

"'Aileen!' It was my uncle, calling from the doorway. 'The children cry for their mother, and I for my meal.'

"The moment was broken. My aunt gathered her berries and a few fallen branches into her apron, and I picked up the handles of the cart. I delivered the fish to my uncle, and he pulled me away across the field to his cow shed, where I gathered a *bo* to walk back to Mallaig."

Luke looked back at Darrell, and his eyes cleared.

"That was the last time I saw my aunt alive." He made the sign of a cross on his chest.

Darrell opened her mouth to speak and then closed it again. Luke bent his head and struggled to find words. When he looked up again, Darrell could see tears swimming in his eyes.

"I am afraid ye've come too late to save my family from grief, Dara," he said quietly. "But ye still seem to me to be a gift from my mother's sister. She was a good woman, and I loved her dearly."

Darrell frowned. "What do you mean, *was* a good woman. Is she —?"

"Yes," Luke nodded. "She is dead." He dropped his head to his chest. Darrell looked away from him for a moment, to give him a chance to catch his breath. She glanced down thoughtfully at Delaney, with his brown fur singed to the skin on one side. When she looked back, Luke's head was held high and his eyes were blazing.

"Shortly before that visit to my aunt, I had been apprenticed to a soldier from the guard at Ainslie Castle. My days were very full and I forgot all about the conversation with my aunt. Nearly a year had passed since my visit to Arisaig, and I was cleaning out the stable where my soldier kept his horse one morning before I went to my apprenticeship at the castle. The day was misty and grey, and I heard a horseman ride through the village, ringing a bell. I could not hear his words, but my father came in the stable at a run and jumped on the horse.

"'There's trouble!' he shouted. 'Stay with yer mother and the bairn.'

"I ran into the house, but my mother was feeding the baby and had not heard the horseman. When my father returned that night, I met him as he rubbed down the horse, which was covered in foam. I was very worried because he had taken the soldier's horse and it was only by luck that the soldier hadn't called for his mount that day. My father would not go in to see my mother until he had washed in the Loch. He stunk of smoke and he was covered in ash. When he returned from the Loch, I heard my mother scream and I ran to her, but he stopped me at the door.

"'Leave her to her wailing, lad.' We walked back to the stables.

"My father gave a forkful of straw to the horse. 'This is a terrible thing, when the witches and faeries take the life a good woman and a mother.'

"'What d'ya mean, Da?'

"'I mean yer auntie is dead, lad, and worse. She was burned for witchcraft, with Logan's missus and another wee old one.'

"My stomach clenched and I gritted my teeth to stop from losing my supper on the straw.

"'What happened?'

"'Och … I'm not sure. I think it had to do with the wee charms she made. She knew too often when the milk would turn sour or the chickens would stop laying. Now that the sickness is sweeping the village, they blame her, and the people have turned on the women who helped them in the past.' He shrugged. 'Tis a terrible shame that the rain held off. If I'd been there an hour before, perhaps I'd have had time to get her away. When I got there the flames were high above the post they'd been tied to, and the smell of burning pitch and flesh was the worst I've ever known.'

"I felt filled with fury. 'What about her husband? Where was he?'

"'I found him in the house, badly beaten, with the bairns around him wailing. By then I'd paid a man to bury Aileen in his field and sent in a local village woman to feed the children.'

"He stood up then, and looked at me. 'This is a terrible sickness, Luke, and I need to find a way to see my wife and children safe.'"

Luke cleared his throat and looked at Darrell. "That was many weeks ago. My father took his fishing boat out alone and we have not seen him again. He never sails alone ... always with two or three other fishermen." Luke bowed his head. "I am sure he is dead ... drowned looking for a place safe for his family away from the sickness."

Darrell patted his shoulder awkwardly, with her heart pounding in her chest. "You couldn't know this, but my own father died three years ago."

Luke shook his head and crossed himself again. "I did not know it, Dara. I am sorry for the loss." He gestured at the wooden peg that stuck out from the hem of her skirt. "Ye've suffered much in yer life," he said softly.

Darrell nodded. "As have you." She turned away to give Luke a chance to wipe his eyes, her mind racing. "Let me get this straight," she said. "Your aunt was burned as a witch because she foretold a tragedy to come. Your family has been hurt. Your village and Arisaig ..." She paused and looked up suddenly. "Luke, you said that many people are sick and dying?"

Luke nodded, mutely.

Darrell rubbed the crease between her eyebrows and spoke sharply. "Is anyone in your family ill?"

Luke nodded, miserably. "My whole family in Arisaig has died," he said bitterly, and swiped at his eyes with the back of his hand. "The flames that took my mother's sister and the two other women did not help. People have begun to sicken everywhere. My aunt's husband, overcome with grief and shame, hid in his home. After a week he too became ill and died in a matter of days. All his children, my cousins, followed him to their graves soon after." Luke paused for breath and looked into the fire.

"Now even here in our small village, the bodies are piling up so fast that they are no longer being given Christian burial. The dead are burned every morning in a place near the centre of the village." He shook his head. "So many have died that soon there will be no one left to do the burning. It is as if Death himself walks among us."

Darrell started. She put her hand into the pocket of the brown skirt and felt a telltale shape there. She drew the object out.

"The woodcut print..."

She looked carefully at the picture that she had been given by Professor Tooth at the start of the summer term. The grim images of the dead and dying stared mutely out from the woodcut. Echoes of Professor Tooth's words chased through her mind. *Epidemic...Plague...Black Death*. Among the bodies in the print, the rats foraged, gnawing bones. And slithering like a snake through the back of her brain came the memory of Professor Tooth's lesson ... and a boy named Luke, dead at nineteen of the Black Plague.

"It's the bubonic plague," she whispered and began to pace. In spite of all that had happened, she felt that there must be some small thing that she could do to help Luke before she tried to find her own way back to Eagle Glen. She put her hand to her head.

"Think, think, think," she muttered. "What do I remember about the plague?" She racked her brain to remember all she had learned from Professor Tooth about the Middle Ages. She looked sharply at Luke. "Do you think I could take a walk around the village with you?" she said suddenly. "I need to see this for myself." Luke nodded. Darrell started toward the door, but halted in her tracks. She whirled toward Luke. "I know you lost your family in Arisaig," she said slowly, "And I am very sorry for your loss. But has anyone who lives in this house become ill?"

Luke shook his head. "My father has been gone since the death of my aunt. My mother has been in mourning for her sister and has not left the house." He gestured at the ceiling. "She sleeps now, with my baby sister, upstairs." He gave a wry grin. "For y'see, my

Auntie Aileen did have the sight … and she saw rightly. I did end up with a baby sister."

"Oh …" Darrell didn't know what to say. A feeling was growing inside her, something she recognized as determination. She realized she had to deal with one thing at a time, and pushed the thoughts of Luke's aunt to the back of her mind with the other things she could not find time to explain.

"I think the most important job right now is to avoid getting sick ourselves. If this really is the time of the plague, most useful drugs won't have been invented yet." She thought for a moment, then turned back to Luke. She looked critically at his clothes. "Do you have any, er, *cleaner* clothes or rags around the house?"

Luke shook his head for a moment, and then brightened. "My sister's christening robes! They are safely wrapped to save for the next child." He ran to a cupboard and rummaged, drawing out a grimy package wrapped in heavy woollen cloth and twine. Darrell watched him doubtfully as he unwrapped the package, but was pleased to see a delicate baby garment, clearly made of silk or some other fine fabric, emerge from the grimy wrappings.

"That will be perfect, Luke. Now, I'm sorry, but we need to cut it up."

Luke looked horrified. "Oh, no, my mother would never allow it. It is our family's most precious possession, next to the rosary." He pointed to a string of beautiful rosewood beads surrounding a pewter cross that hung on the wall near the fireplace.

"I'm very sorry," Darrell repeated firmly, "but if we are to save your family, it is completely necessary." She picked up a knife from the large table and began to slice up the fine cloth. Luke crossed himself once more and looked guiltily toward the ladder that led to the upper storey where his mother and sister slept. In moments, Darrell had fashioned two face masks, similar to those her mother wore during surgical procedures at the hospital.

"These are a bit rough," she said as she tied one around Luke's face, "but they'll do for our quick tour of the village." She fastened her own mask over her nose and mouth and tied it firmly behind her head.

"Let me take your arm, so I don't trip over this stupid leg," she said to Luke. "And if anyone asks, say that I am one of your remaining cousins from Arisaig. That should keep people far enough away."

Delaney trotting behind, they stepped out into the dark lane.

Chapter Seven

As they walked through the streets of Mallaig, Darrell
knew she was walking through a dark chapter of history. The village was small, only a couple of short lanes
surrounding a village square. The few people they saw
usually scurried out of their way, frightened, perhaps,
by the masks she and Luke wore. Darrell was struck by
the tiny size of most of the people she saw. She was certainly taller than anyone she had seen except Luke,
who was about her size. The smell of the streets was
dank and rancid, though the masks made it somewhat
easier to bear.

"How old are you, Luke?" Darrell asked, with
curiosity.

"In October I will enter my twentieth year," he said
proudly. Darrell was surprised. She had thought Luke,
by his dress and manner, to be about thirteen, her own

age. Instead, she found he was a fully grown man. Another question nagged at her.

"Luke," Darrell said carefully. "Try not to think I'm out of my mind, but I have — ah — been out of the country for a while and I am not sure of the date. Do you keep track of the date?"

"I, too, am not sure of the exact date," Luke replied. "I do know it is sometime in early summer, in the year of our Lord thirteen hundred and fifty."

Darrell had to stop and catch her breath for a moment. Everything had pointed to this, but she was still having trouble grasping the reality of all she could see around her. Somehow, she had journeyed more than six hundred years back in time.

She looked around the village as it spread out around her. It was primarily small buildings, many with straw roofs and wattle and daub construction. The streets were cobbled, and a few thin horses and oxen could be seen, generally pulling carts. She did not notice anybody riding horses; most walked at the heads of their animals as they pulled carts loaded with straw or rocks. A few skinny dogs ran through the lanes, and one ran up to bark at Delaney.

Darrell was startled by the contrast between Delaney and the other dogs. In spite of Delaney's thin and dirty appearance, he still had a gleam in his eye and a jaunt to his tail. The barking dog was gaunt, obviously starving. Darrell could see every bone of his spine protruding through the painfully thin fur on his back. Even his bark lacked vigour, and he turned and crept away at a quiet word from Luke.

A couple of fat cats slunk by, and after the scrawny dogs the sight almost made Darrell smile. *At least the cats are doing well,* she thought, with some irony.

The cobbled lanes were filthy, with gutters running with sewage. Twice, Darrell and Luke had to scurry out of the way as women threw washtubs of dirty water into the street, and once they narrowly missed being hit by a load of kitchen garbage tossed out a window.

"Where are all the ill people?" Darrell asked.

"As people fall ill, they return to their homes to die. The dead are taken to the village square to be burned."

Darrell swallowed. "Could we go there?"

Luke looked disgusted. "Why there? All ye'll see are the dead, and many flies and rats. Even the village gravedigger cannot help ye, because he too has died of this terrible plague."

"I don't want to go in, I just want to have a look at the place. I need to be sure that I'm right." Luke agreed reluctantly, and they made their way toward the village square.

They could smell the place long before they could see it. The masks that they had donned earlier were no help against the stench of death and burning. Luke would not enter the square, but stopped and leaned against a wall. Darrell, fighting the urge to retch, walked closer to the home of the now deceased gravedigger.

Three bodies lay on the ground, looking pitiful and small in death, mercifully hidden under old sacking. But as Darrell watched, a man staggered into the yard, bearing a small bundle in his arms.

"Someone help me," he called piteously. "Please help me! My child is not well."

Darrell instinctively stepped out into the square, but a woman brushed her aside and bustled up to the man.

"I'll take her, Alexander. Ye need to sit down and rest. Please, sit here, I will get ye a drink."

The man turned grateful eyes on the woman as he slid to sit on a rough-hewn wooden bench outside the house. "Please check her, Abbie," he said hoarsely. "I think her breathing is better now. She is resting more easily."

Darrell watched as the woman laid the tiny lifeless body beside the other three on the ground.

"I'm sure she'll be fine, Alexander," Abbie said soothingly. "Let's walk ye home, to get some rest." She gave the man a drink and then led him out of the square, supporting him on her shoulder as she passed Darrell and Luke. Darrell could hear the laboured breathing of the man as he walked by and could see the telltale swelling under his jaw. The woman's eyes met Darrell's as they passed, and she smiled kindly, though she herself looked ready to drop.

"She is Abbie, the village midwife," whispered Luke, after they had passed. "How she is still on her feet after treating so many of the sick, I cannot say."

Darrell and Luke started back to his house. She could not get the sight of the small body left on the ground out of her mind. The baby's skin had been so blue it looked almost black, and the throat had been swollen grotesquely.

Luke was clearly thinking the same thing. "Alexander is the village cobbler," he said. "That baby was born the same month as Rose." He sighed. "Abbie helped Alexander's wife deliver the baby, and then she came to help my mother."

Darrell was rocked by the enormity of this tragedy. When she had learned in Professor Tooth's class that as many as one in every two people had died in the most affected parts of Europe, it had only been numbers. Seeing the faces and the agony of the loss of family and friends this close was almost too much to bear.

Darrell cleared her throat and said roughly, "I've seen enough. I want to go back to speak with your mother, Luke."

As they made their way quickly back to Luke's small dwelling, Darrell could see the turrets of a castle, cast in light stone, on a distant knoll surrounded by the water of the loch.

"What is that place?" she asked Luke in surprise.

"That is Ainslie Castle, the ancestral seat of the clan MacKenzie. The lands around the village all belong to the Laird."

"Are you his servants, then?"

"No, my family are fishermen, but many peasants work his fields and are beholden to him for their lives and livelihood." He thought for a moment. "We were very lucky, before this tragedy. The Laird is a fair man and usually was good to the people who worked for him. Many neighbouring areas do not have as strong a protector. The castle is on a tidal island, and when the tide is in, it is protected by the waters of the loch."

"Where is the Laird now?" asked Darrell.

"I heard he travels to the far north, to the Nordic lands, where they say the Black Death has not yet found its way."

Darrell sighed impatiently. "Some benefactor," she said, scornfully.

"Oh, but he has left behind the castle guard to maintain order in his absence," replied Luke. "They are a fine group of soldiers who help to keep the peace." He dropped his head modestly. "It is my goal to join them one day, but first I must be apprenticed to another of the guard."

"Another guard? Weren't you an apprentice already?"

Luke nodded eagerly as he steered them in the direction of his home. "Yes, and I have learned much, about arms and warfare, animal husbandry, and how carefully to keep a soldier's kit." His expression became more serious. "The guard under whose tutelage I studied was taken by the illness several weeks ago. His death has left me without a patron."

Darrell nodded, her mind preoccupied with both the struggle to walk without slipping on the cobblestone lane and the magnitude of the tragedy looming around her.

That night, Darrell sat down to eat with Luke, his mother, Maggie, and his baby sister, Rose. Luke introduced Darrell to his mother as Dara, a friend of Maggie's sister from Arisaig, and she clung to Darrell and sobbed her grief into Darrell's shoulder. Luke's mother had circles under her pale grey eyes and her black hair was shot through with strands of pure white.

Darrell helped Maggie to a seat by the fire and then gently explained the plan she had come up with that afternoon, during her tour of the village with Luke.

"I would like to see your family safe," Darrell explained. "We cannot halt the spread of this terrible disease, but perhaps we can preserve the lives of Luke and Rose."

Luke's mother looked like she was going to cry again, so Darrell spoke hastily. "Is there anything left for you here?" she asked. Maggie shook her head mutely.

"I have sold all we had to pay for the burial of my sister," she wept. "They would not allow her to be buried on sanctified ground, and my husband had to pay a man to bury her in a field."

"Do you know how dangerous this disease is to you?" Darrell asked.

Maggie nodded. "The sickness has taken all," she said, despairingly. "We are in God's hands now."

Darrell shook her head. "I think I can help you. I have some knowledge that I learned when I was — ah — abroad. This disease is transmitted by fleas on rats and people. When the people get sick, it goes into their lungs. They cough and that can make others ill, too. If you want to keep well," she continued, "you must stay far away from those who are sick. Do you have somewhere else you can go, to a place in the country, perhaps, where the illness has not made its way, yet?"

Luke spoke up. "Father's family is from the northernmost part of the Highlands, far from here. It is a journey of many days, perhaps weeks, but we would be welcome there."

"Then you must go," said Darrell firmly. "And when you get there, you must keep the house very clean." She gestured at the floor. "You have to get rid of rushes like these on the floor. When food and crumbs fall in here, it draws rats." She looked doubtfully at the clothes Maggie and Luke were wearing.

"Maggie, you must try to keep your family's bodies clean. You must try to bathe in a stream or tub every day, and scrub away the lice and insects that live in your clothes or on your skin."

Maggie looked startled. She looked at Luke in some confusion. He turned to Darrell to try to explain.

"Ye must understand that clothing is very expensive and that our father is only a poor fisherman. When the weather gets cool, our mother takes our underclothes and sews them in place. We wear them for the whole winter: when we sleep, for warmth, and when we rise, under our outer clothing."

Darrell turned to Luke impatiently. "You must listen to me. This is why so many people are dying. This plague has made its way from somewhere in China on ships to devastate all of Europe. The disease is borne in the bloodstream of fleas that live on the bodies of rats. The rats run from ship to shore and spread the illness when the fleas jump onto humans."

Luke looked despairing. "This is a port village. The rats run everywhere, here. Ye saw them yerself this afternoon."

Darrell spoke firmly. "All the more reason to go to the north. It is away from the water, and if the disease has reached the area, you can keep it out of the home of your relatives by keeping rats and fleas to a minimum, and trying to keep your bodies free of dirt and insects."

Maggie stood up and placed the sleeping Rose into her small cradle. She turned to look at Darrell and Luke, and her eyes flashed.

"This angel from Arisaig has been sent to us by my beloved sister. These are strange ideas she brings, but I believe her. We will leave word for yer father to seek us with his family in the north. We will leave tomorrow." She looked around. "Ye spoke truly, Dara. There is nothing left for us here."

She turned to Darrell and hugged her gently, and this time there were no tears in her eyes.

"Ye have given me hope, *mo cridhe*," Maggie whispered, "and that is more than I have had in a very long time."

Luke made a bed for Darrell on a bench after the two of them had spent more than an hour first sweeping and then washing the floor clean. Delaney curled up on the floor beside her and dozed by the fire. Darrell slept little that night, her thoughts whirling through her head. The next day, she helped the family pack a small cart with their belongings. As the afternoon wore on, she said goodbye to Maggie with hope that she and her children would survive where others had not.

As Luke finished strapping a final few treasures into the wagon, he looked up at Darrell with a strange glint in his eye. He dashed back into the small house while Maggie settled Rose in a sling around her shoulders. A moment later, he emerged and thrust something hurriedly into Darrell's hand.

"This belonged to my aunt. She told me to take it if I had stomach trouble. It is the last one. Ye must have it." His blue eyes glowed warmly in Darrell's for a moment and then he turned away and lifted the handles of the heavy cart. Darrell looked with puzzlement at the small piece of toffee that Luke had dropped into her palm. She looked up in time to watch them, faces masked against infection, trudge away down the same dark lane that she had walked up only yesterday. It was not until she waved a last goodbye to Luke that she remembered that she, too, had a journey to make.

She turned and limped wearily down the lane, toward the sea and the rocky cave that she hoped would take her home. The wooden peg rubbed painfully on the stump of her leg, and with every step she took, her worries grew. What would happen to Luke and his family? How could the flimsy masks they wore protect them from the virulent illness that swept through this devastated land? The peg thumped gently on the filthy cobblestones, and she held her hand up to block most of the smell from the reeking stream that swept along beside the road. Delaney's collar jangled gently as he trotted along beside her, the sound rising now as she hurried and he ran to keep up.

She stopped abruptly and looked down at Delaney, who halted obediently at her side and gazed up at her with a grin. His ears slid forward and he turned his head to look back the way they had come.

"Your collar can't be jingling ..." Darrell began, but by that time the noise was so loud that all thoughts of Delaney's absent collar were driven from her mind. There was a shout behind her, and two uniformed horsemen rode up in a clash of armour, the horses' hooves striking sparks against the cobbles.

Darrell silently cursed herself for the preoccupation that kept her mind too busy to hear the arrival of the soldiers until it was too late to duck into a shadowy doorway.

"Hold!" There was no mistaking the command in the soldier's voice. Darrell's chin lifted defiantly. Dismounted, the soldier was almost a full head shorter than she, and he looked far less threatening than when mounted. The soldiers wore leather tunics over woollen shirts, and atop the tunics they wore vests of dirty chain mail. Through the chain she could see that they both had a similar crest painted on the breast of their leather tunics, though it was getting too dark to make out the design.

"I have no intention of holding," she said shortly, thinking fast. "My aunt is expecting me and I must return home before nightfall." She started to turn away, but the soldier took her arm with a grip that belied his small stature.

"Ow!" she cried and tried unsuccessfully to pull her arm away.

"Looks like ye've found yerself a fine specimen," chuckled the mounted soldier to his compatriot. He glanced admiringly at Darrell. "Look at the height of this woman! She will surely be able to accomplish the work of two. The Laird would be pleased."

Unable to tear her arm out of the grasp of the soldier, Darrell bit her lip, balanced on her sore stump, and stomped on the soldier's foot. Though he wore a tall leather riding boot, it did not have a reinforced toe, and it became his turn to cry out. He leaped back in some surprise but did not release his grip, and Darrell was pulled off balance. Unable to keep upright on the slippery cobbles, she crashed into the small soldier. The weight of his armour proved too much; he tipped over, and the two of them landed in an untidy heap, only just missing the brown stream that ran alongside the road.

The soldier regained his feet in a moment, spluttering and fuming, his face red. His mounted companion laughed heartily from his saddle. Darrell had a more difficult time, for the road was slimy with unnamed filth, and her wooden peg slipped on the greasy surface. The small soldier offered no assistance, but had mercifully let go his vise-like grip on her arm.

By the time she stood up, Darrell's whole body felt sore. Her leg throbbed where it was bound to the peg, and her arm was bruised and aching. She looked down to see her sleeve was almost torn away, and the tanned skin of her arm showed through the rent in the fabric.

The mounted soldier stopped laughing and gestured to his companion. "Time to move on, Hamish. It is getting late, and we need to find one or two more before dark."

The small soldier frowned. "I say we take this one. She is strong and healthy. Look at her teeth! She shows no sign of the sickness."

The mounted soldier barked a short, humourless laugh. "Hamish, look at her! She is a cripple. She has probably been shunned by her family for her deformity." He spat onto the ground near Darrell's feet, and she hurriedly stepped away, stumbling a bit on the cobbles. "The castle needs strong work horses right now. She is useless."

In the distance a shout rose up. Darrell looked back up the cobbled lane. Dusk was stealing the light and it was hard to see anything clearly. A light glimmered in the distance and then flared as a torch was lit, and then two. Out of the gloom, a third horse came flying down the lane toward them, bearing yet another soldier. Darrell's heart began to pound. The soldier stopped halfway down the lane and called out.

"Captain! Julian! Fall in! We have found a family that will meet our needs." He turned and galloped back to the group of soldiers.

The mounted soldier glanced down at Darrell. She winced as she tried to avoid putting weight on her sore leg. "Leave the cripple."

The small soldier hesitated and smiled up at his companion, showing a mouthful of brown and broken teeth. "She may be no use at the Castle," he said slyly, "but I'm sure we could find ... something ... for her to do." He sneered at Darrell and grabbed her bare arm, pinching her cruelly. Darrell tugged her arm and cried out in frustration at the soldiers, who were now both leering at her.

The light at the end of the lane suddenly blazed as many torches were lit at once. Darrell could see with sickening clarity that a large group of soldiers, all with tunics similar to those worn by the men who stood with her, had surrounded Luke and his family. As the light flared, a brown blur flew past her face and a voice cried out in pain. The horse that bore the mounted soldier reared suddenly, and Darrell found she was free. The small soldier lay on the cobbles once more, bleeding freely from a bite on his leg and in danger of being trampled by his companion's horse. Delaney ran between the horses, nipping at their hocks and nimbly avoiding the crashing hooves. The horse reared and the mounted soldier was thrown, landing like a heap on top of the small soldier on the ground. Angry shouts and confusion reigned.

Darrell, taking advantage of the momentary chaos, gritted her teeth and fled down the stone steps to the beach, pain flaming in her leg like the torches in the lane behind her. Delaney ran beside her, still a brown blur in the dim twilight of the cloudy evening. As she ran down the beach, she could hear the clink of armour from a pursuing soldier. Darrell kept running until she neared the rocks and it became too difficult to see the hard-packed surface of the beach. With the copper taste of fear fresh in her mouth, she stopped to look back at the stone steps only to see a burning torch bobbing along the beach behind her.

Gasping, and with searing pain in every step, Darrell limped along the rocky outcropping, moving out toward the water. She was sick with worry, both for Luke and for her own well-being.

I can't run much further, she thought in a haze of pain. *How am I ever going to find the cave with no light?* She looked down the vast wall of rock with its many notches, crags, and indentations spreading over several hundred metres of beach.

Delaney snuffled his nose into Darrell's hand and whined.

"Find the cave, Delaney," Darrell whispered desperately. A few metres ahead of her, Delaney barked and appeared to veer into the rock face. Darrell glanced at the torch-bearing soldier behind her. He was at least fifty metres away still, but she could hear his breath, ragged with the effort of chasing her.

Darrell stepped hurriedly around the pile of boulders at the cave entrance.

"Good dog, Delaney!" she whispered and followed him inside.

Outside she could hear a muffled curse as the soldier lost sight of her. Inside the cave, the darkness was absolute, and Darrell once again had to make her way through touch. With her left hand held out straight in front to protect her face, she walked as quickly as she could, running her right hand along the rough, wet surface of the wall. The rock wall was jagged, and she scraped her knuckles more than once on barnacles that lined the cave. After five minutes of slow progress, she stopped for breath. She could hear Delaney panting cheerfully up ahead.

Darrell's stomach was twisted in a knot of worry for Luke, Maggie, and baby Rose. Where would the soldiers be taking them? She felt wracked with guilt for running away. *I have to figure how to get Luke and his family out of this mess,* she thought. She slid down the cave wall to sit on the sand, only to find the ground was wet. Really wet. The tide was rising and water had begun to flow into the cave.

That's why I was scraping my knuckles on barnacles, thought Darrell. *This can't be the right place. The other cave was completely dry.* Aloud, she called out, "Delaney! I don't want to get stuck in here by the tide. Come on, boy, let's turn around." The thought of the soldier on the beach chilled her, but there had to be somewhere she could hide where she wouldn't drown in the meantime.

Darrell had put her weight back on to her sore leg with a groan when she heard Delaney whimper behind her.

"Delaney, come!" she said firmly, but she heard no answering movement. The water was up above her ankle now and she felt a pang of worry.

"Delaney! Please come!" No dog.

Resolutely, she hiked up the hem of her now sodden wool skirt and headed deeper into the cave. She reached downward to feel for Delaney with her left hand and continued to hold the wall with her right. In less than a minute, she felt a warm nose snuffle into her hand.

"Thank goodness you're okay, Delaney," she sighed with relief. "Now let's get out of here." But Delaney continued to whine, and Darrell was forced to drop to her knees in the water to see if she could feel what was wrong with the dog. The cold water swirling around her thighs made her gasp, but it blunted the pain in her leg for a moment or two and she sighed with relief.

In that moment, her hands felt Delaney's paw, caught under a rock beneath the rapidly rising water. She scrabbled her fingers under the rock and tried to feel if she could pull his paw loose. It was stuck fast.

In desperation, with the water now up to Delaney's chest, she reached up to grab the rock wall for purchase. As she clutched her arm around Delaney's neck, her hand slipped and both of them plunged under water. His paw wrenched free, but before she could even feel relief, a sudden sharp shock ran through her body and she found that she could no longer breathe.

CHAPTER EIGHT

When the world stopped spinning, Darrell found she could not sit up. She lay where she was, head swimming and gut churning, then rolled over and was quietly sick on the sand. She got up onto her knees and crawled two or three steps away from the mess, and then collapsed back onto the floor of the cave. Her body felt like someone had beaten her with a board all over. Twice.

She curled in a ball on the sand and listened to the distant lapping of the surf on the beach. It was a calming, quiet sound and it, more than anything, helped her to come back to herself. Her mouth tasted terrible. She made a move to roll over on the sand and felt a bump like a small pebble under her leg. She reached down to push it out of the way and realized that whatever it was, it was in her pocket. Since the darkness was absolute she lay on her back and felt the object with her fingers. Small, round — it was the candy that Luke had given her.

Darrell remembered Luke saying something about an upset stomach. She slipped the candy into her mouth and rolled gingerly onto her side. The sweet taste was welcome. The nausea receded almost immediately, and she found herself able to think once more.

As soon as her memory returned, she struggled to sit up. Even with her eyes wide open, she was unable to see what she was wearing or if Delaney was anywhere near. The sudden movement had made her head swim again briefly, but this time the feeling was shorter-lived. A faint red glow illuminated the inside of the cave and she looked up in time to see the image of a tree burning like a red brand on the rocky wall. As she watched, the glow faded like a dying ember into darkness.

Though wisps of wet hair clung to her face and neck, the rest of her was completely dry. She ran her hands down her legs and could feel sand-covered cotton. Her jeans!

Darrell whispered, "Delaney," her voice hoarse and sore. She made a move to go forward and found her path blocked by a soft, warm body.

"Delaney!" He answered her with a lick across the cheek. She felt relief washing through her at the feel of his fur under her fingers accompanied by the warm, familiar smell of wet dog. She patted him gently and gingerly stood up, careful not to bump her head on a rock outcropping. Using her fingers along the wall as a guide, she crab-walked sideways up the gently sloping floor of the cave, making her way toward the sound of the sea.

Darrell walked for less than five minutes before she was able to detect a change in the light. The walls were first black shadows and then grey. In the dim light, she saw her pack tucked safely behind a rock where she had left it and gratefully slipped it on. She crept forward slowly, not at all sure of what to expect.

From the light pouring through the crack in the rock wall above the entrance to the cave, Darrell could see it was daytime. She remembered her watch and looked at it curiously. She was sure that the shocks that had shot through her arm before she travelled must have stopped the mechanism, but when she looked at it, it appeared to be working. She shook it and looked again. It must have stopped and re-started, because it registered only twenty minutes as having passed since she was first jerked through the wall of time. She thought for a moment and realized that she had slept overnight at the home of Luke's family, so at least twenty-four hours had passed. Darrell checked the date on her watch. It read yesterday's date. That proved it. The watch must have stopped sometime during the first few moments of the journey.

Darrell crept carefully to the entrance to peek out and ensure that no one would notice her coming out of the cave. She peered out, squinting, as her eyes got used to the bright sunlight. In the distance, she could see Lily and Andrea, her swimming partner, wade, shivering, into the waters of the bay. No one else was in sight. She stepped cautiously out through the tiny crevice that formed the mouth of the cave. Her head reeled and she put her hand on the rock wall for a moment to steady herself, fearing a return of the terrible nausea.

It doesn't smell the same here as in Mallaig, she thought with a pang. *The light's different, too.*

She rubbed her forehead wearily. *Maybe it's me that's changed.* Her stomach clenched at the thought of all she had left behind in Mallaig. What would happen to Maggie and Rose? The shouts of the soldiers rang in her ears with sickening clarity. *Coward!* she thought bitterly. *I should have tried to help them somehow.* Her feet dragging, she stepped onto the beach.

As she walked by the boulders, she noticed that none of the small white plastic boxes remained. After what she had been through in the last twenty-four hours, suddenly Conrad's activities seemed much less important. Still … it was a shame she had missed the perfect opportunity to capture Conrad on film …

Her stomach dropped into her shoes.

The camera.

"I must have left it in the cave," she muttered and turned to retrace her steps. Inside the cave everything remained the same. The cedar bough was deep in the cave where she had left it, but there was no sign of the camera. She pulled everything out of her backpack.

Nothing. No camera.

Darrell crept back out of the cave, rubbing the crease between her eyebrows. She glanced around again to ensure no one had seen her emerge, and then slowly limped up the beach toward the school.

Her mind whirled with confusion. What was she going to tell everyone about where she had been for twenty-four hours? Where was her camera? Had someone found it? Had Conrad? The sickening possibility that Conrad had found her camera made her stop in her tracks. The film had been exposed, so he would know there was no danger to him, but her name was clearly printed across the back of the case. He would know she had been watching. She suddenly felt very frightened, and very alone.

Lily was waving from her place in the water, and Darrell returned the wave. She was going to need to come up with a good story to cover her absence from the school, and lying was not her strong suit. She paused and leaned against the boulders to think.

"Hey, Darrell, there you are!" Kate was making her way down the winding cliff path from the school, wearing her tae kwon do uniform, a black belt tied tightly around the waist. Darrell felt frantic. She hadn't had time to think up an explanation for her absence. What could she say to Kate?

"I think Brodie's looking for you," said Kate, oblivious to Darrell's panic. "I decided that you guys were right. I've been too much of a tech-head lately, so I'm going to practice some of my tae kwon do patterns on the beach and maybe try a few kicks. You want to stay and watch?"

With an airy wave she walked past Darrell and strode down to the sand near where Lily and her friends were swimming.

Darrell's jaw dropped as she looked at Kate's retreating back. Why hadn't Kate asked where she had been? She didn't have to make up a lie because Kate hadn't asked. She turned and, with her sore leg throbbing, slowly walked up the winding path to the school. As she stepped into the garden behind the school, she spotted her coffee cup, left there the day before.

Darrell realized that she was unbelievably hungry, so she scooped up her coffee cup from the grass and stepped into the kitchen to have something to eat.

After breakfast, Darrell walked up to her room. A painkiller had dampened the worst of her sore leg, but for good measure she sat down on her bed and removed her prosthesis. From her window she could see Lily, out of the water, talking with Kate on the beach.

Darrell picked up her pen and began to write in her notebook. She outlined everything she could remember and added a whole new list of questions to her previous pages. How could she have been drawn back through time? What had happened to Luke and his family? The act of writing made her feel more organized, but she was still not sure that she wasn't losing her mind. It was obvious that she had been gone for at least a day. She had slept in Luke's house overnight. Yet no one here at Eagle Glen had missed her. Her watch showed that less than thirty minutes had passed since she had run deep into the cave to hide from Conrad. Had time compressed in some way? And just where had she been, anyway? Now that she was sitting on her comfortable bed, only the ghost of pain in her leg spoke of her journey through space and time.

Darrell frowned as she remembered the only other time in her life that she had doubted her own sanity. When she awoke from the accident and found herself in a hospital bed, she had spent the better part of a week trying to convince herself it was all a terrible dream. In reality, the fathers of ten-year-old girls did not die in motorcycle accidents. The loss of a father and a leg were things of nightmare, not of real life. But at that terrible time, Darrell had nurses and hospital equipment and the devastated face of her mother to tell her that it had not all been a dream. Now there was no hard evidence at all.

She glanced down at her arm and saw four bruises, blue and distinct through her tan. Fingerprints from another time.

"This is crazy," she said to herself. "I need to forget about this for a while or I'm going to go nuts." She carefully locked her notebook away in her desk drawer, slipped back into her prosthesis, and went down to the art studio.

Darrell pulled an overstuffed chair into the corner and began sketching furiously. She was concentrating so fully on her work that she didn't notice Mr. Gill come in.

"A day like this was meant for working outside, Darrell."

"Oh, hi, Mr. Gill. I — ah — just needed to sit down for a while. I'm a bit — tired from working at night." Her face coloured at the lie.

Arthur Gill did not seem to notice. He was looking at the sketch in Darrell's hand, and then he looked around the room with a puzzled expression.

"What are you sketching from? Have you got a photograph pinned up somewhere?"

She shook her head. "Just from memory."

"A picture you remember seeing, then?"

"Not really."

Mr. Gill looked up from the sketch. "You have captured some amazing detail from just a mental image." He rubbed his jaw as he spoke. "Have you been to some of the older parts of Europe, then? The Vieux Port in Marseilles, or perhaps some part of Prague?"

Darrell could not meet his eyes. Her face burned. She looked down at her sketch of the dark streets she had walked earlier that very day. "Um, yes. I'm not sure where it was actually. It seems like a long time ago, now. It may just be from a picture I have seen somewhere in a book." She cleared her throat and managed to look up. "I just have this image in my mind, and I feel like putting it on paper."

Mr. Gill looked at her quizzically. "What do you plan to do once you have finished the sketch?"

"I have a series of sketches in mind. I think I might paint this one using the acrylics that I was trying out this week," she answered absently, her mind swirling with pictures of Luke and Rose in danger, Maggie in tears.

Mr. Gill looked critically at the sketch. "I sense a strong feeling of darkness in this sketch, Darrell. You may be better off with oils on this one, in order to capture the unique light in the sky." He stood up and started to rustle through cupboards. "I think we have some of the right shades in here," he said, his voice muffled as

133

he rummaged. "I have to go to a portrait appointment today, but," he brought his head out of the cupboard and looked at Darrell, "I am very interested to see what you will come up with. Your sketch looks so alive. I can't wait to see how it turns out when you paint it."

Mr. Gill left a number of supplies out for Darrell and then hurried out of the room to his appointment. She settled back down to her sketching. After about an hour, she gathered her materials and tried to forget her tumbling thoughts by immersing herself up to the elbows in oil paint.

Later in the afternoon the light in the studio deepened, and Darrell's stomach began to rumble. She looked up at the clock on the wall of the studio and noticed with some surprise that it was almost five o'clock. She stood up and stretched to loosen the muscles of her back and arms, then decided to wrap up her work for the day. Her body was sore from being still for so long, but her mind felt much clearer than it had that morning. She decided to have some dinner and then sit down to fig-ure out what to do next.

As she walked down the hall, Mrs. Follett came scurrying out of the door to the office.

"Oh, Darrell! I'm glad I've found you so quickly. There is a telephone call for you in the office. I think it's your mother. Hurry on in, dear, you can take it at my desk."

Darrell stepped into the office and picked up the phone with some concern.

"Hi, Mom. Is everything all right?"

Dr. Connor's cheerful voice came over the line. "Hi, honey. That was the very question I was going to ask you! My flight got in two hours ago and I've just made it home. I have so much to tell you about Europe. It was fantastic!" Dr. Connor lowered her voice. "But, Darrell, I had the strangest feeling the whole time I was away that you were having a terrible time at Eagle Glen, so I decided that the moment I got home I would call you. I have to go back to work on Monday, but I could come up tomorrow and bring you home, if that's what you want."

"NO!" Darrell realized she was shouting and spoke more quietly. "Sorry, Mom, I didn't mean to yell. It's just that I'm — well — I'm having a really … interesting time here, and I'm just not ready to leave yet."

"Darling! That is wonderful news. And here I was, thinking that you were hating the place. I felt like such a gorgon leaving you there, when you were so unhappy."

"Oh, well, it's turned out to be a pretty — ah — unusual school, Mom. The art teacher, Mr. Gill, is great. He's helping me paint up a storm and giving me a lot of pointers on technique. And did you know that

135

Professor Tooth teaches history? I've been taking her classes, and she's been telling us a lot about the history of art and how artists throughout history depicted people's lives. It's just, I don't know — just more interesting than I thought it would be."

"Darrell, I can't tell you how different you sound." Janice Connor's voice faltered. "It's as if the old Darrell's come back — the Darrell that I used to know. Oh, I don't know what I'm saying." She sniffed audibly. "You just sound so happy and that makes me happy, too. Just remember that I'm home now and anytime you have had enough, I can come up and get you, okay?"

"Okay, Mom. The way things are, I think I can probably stick it out until the end of the summer." She paused. "I do miss you, though. It's really good to hear your voice."

"You too, my love. Call me anytime, okay?"

"Thanks, Mom. I'll talk to you soon."

Darrell walked slowly out of the office, thinking about how much had changed since the last time she had seen her mother. She remembered sitting in a history lesson when Professor Tooth had read a quotation from William Shakespeare's famous play *Macbeth*:

If you can look into the seeds of time,
And say which grain will grow and which will not ...

Professor Tooth had asked them to think of all the different things that happened in the past as seeds. She had said that some seeds grow, becoming the future, and that some never grow at all. Then she asked the class to think about what they would change about the past if they could. Since the lesson had been about the Middle Ages, most of the kids talked about changing the terrible things that had happened in the past, like the invention of weapons and the beginning of wars or the spread of disease.

Images of Luke and his family surrounded by soldiers filled Darrell's mind. But slowly another thought took shape. What if Darrell could change that fateful day when she and her dad had gone for a drive in the mountains for ice cream? What if they'd had a flat tire and couldn't go? What if she had been sick and forced to stay in bed? How much would that have changed *her* future? She pulled out her notebook and jotted the question down, to think about later.

Deep in thought, Darrell walked into the dining room at the same time as Brodie and Kate. They chose their food from the buffet table and sat down together to eat.

Kate looked tired and happy. "I've spent the whole afternoon sparring with Boris Meirz."

Brodie looked puzzled.

"You know, he's taking one of my computer programming classes, but mostly he practices chess. Anyway, it turns out he has a brown belt in judo. The discipline is quite different from tae kwon do," she went on cheerfully, between mouthfuls of chili, "but it was still pretty fun to work out at that level of intensity."

Brodie had hardly touched his dinner. Darrell watched Kate wolf down two bowls of chili in less than five minutes. She looked quizzically at Brodie. "Not hungry?"

He looked up, startled out of his reverie. "Oh — yeah, yeah, I'm hungry." He picked up his spoon and then appeared to make up his mind about something.

"It's just — well, I found something today." He reached into the backpack at his feet and handed Darrell an object.

Her camera.

Darrell looked up at him and could not read what she saw in his eyes. Was it excitement? Fear? She felt so relieved that Brodie had been the one to find her camera, not Conrad. But this opened a whole new worry. How much did Brodie know?

Brodie looked around to see who was nearby. The three of them sat alone at a table and there didn't appear to be anyone within earshot.

He spoke in a low voice. "I have something to tell you guys. I wasn't sure if I would keep it to myself, but really it was because of you that I found it." He looked at Darrell.

"Because of her? Found what?" Kate asked, now attacking an enormous piece of chocolate cake.

Brodie laughed. "Man, you sure can eat!"

Kate looked hurt. "I've had a busy day, okay? Now tell us what you found."

Brodie looked again at Darrell. "Well," he said slowly, "I'm not sure you didn't find it first." When she didn't answer, he continued. "This morning I heard a boat revving its engines and it woke me up early. So I went out to look again at the rock face where we found all the fossils. I was walking along the wall when I caught sight of something long and black that looked like it was sticking out of rocks. It was the strap of your camera, lying on the sand at a crevice in the wall. I squeezed through the crevice and found a cave."

Kate gasped. "That is *so* great, Brodie. Did you go inside?"

"Yeah, and it *was* really great." He turned to Darrell. "When I saw the strap belonged to a camera with your name on it, I went back to the school to find you and give it back. But I couldn't find you anywhere, and I couldn't stand the thought of that unexplored cave, so I went back with a flashlight and spent the day checking it out."

Darrell made a quick decision. She told Kate and Brodie of her suspicions about Conrad, and about her early-morning adventure in the cave, carefully omitting what had happened afterward. They both looked shocked.

"So I must have dropped my camera when I was leaving after they had driven away in their boat, Brodie. Thank you for finding it for me."

Brodie frowned. "I'm sorry to tell you this, but the back was open. Any pictures that you got of Conrad must have been ruined."

Kate looked exasperated. "Next time you decide to go capture someone on film, Darrell, let me know. My digital camera works on a disk, and you can't lose any pictures by exposing a film. Besides," she added, looking sternly at Darrell, "you need to tell us when you are doing something that dangerous. If he had caught you, who knows what could have happened? It would have been safer to have us there too."

Brodie laughed. "Safer to have Kate there, anyway! I've got to learn some of those moves you put on Connie the last time, Kate. He didn't really have any choice but to hit the dirt!"

While Brodie and Kate were bantering, a strange feeling came over Darrell. She realized that they had both just expressed concern for her welfare. They had been interested in her story and worried about her safety. She watched them teasing each other while Kate ate a second piece of cake. Maybe she could ask them for their help, not just with Conrad but with her dilemma about the special cave. She started to open her mouth when Brodie turned back to her.

"So what do you think, Darrell. Want to come with me?"

Darrell reddened. "Sorry, I must have been daydreaming. Go with you where?"

"Back to the cave. I found these amazing old glyphs written on the wall near the back of the cave where it becomes impassable." He dropped his voice. "This could be something really big, Darrell. A true archaeological find. I really want to look at it some more before I tell Professor Dickerman."

"Did you touch the symbols, or whatever you called them?" asked Darrell, fear in her voice.

Brodie scoffed. "Glyphs. Ancient symbols used before there were really any written words. And of course I didn't touch them. You don't touch things like that. They are so old that they could crumble to dust. What I'd really like to do," he continued, "is to go back with the proper equipment to take a tiny sample. My friend Zack's brother goes to university. He's studying archaeology and he may be able to do some carbon dating on the sample."

He paused and looked pleadingly at Darrell and Kate. "I'd really like to keep this find a secret for now."

"No problem," said Kate without hesitation. "But tomorrow, I have to finish this tricky programming glitch I've run into." She smiled ruefully and gestured at the window. The sky had clouded ominously. "And we've all got that essay for Professor Tooth. It doesn't really look like good outdoor weather, anyway. I need to keep my face glued to my computer screen for a few days."

"Yeah, well, I don't have the proper equipment here, anyway." Brodie's lips thinned with disappointment for a moment, then he brightened. "I'll call my brother. He should be able to send me the stuff I need in a few days. I'd better make a list..." He whipped out a sheet of paper and rapidly jotted a few notes.

Darrell felt troubled. She hated to share the cave with anyone, but it now was out of her hands. It was Brodie's cave now, too. She just had to keep him from touching the symbols on the wall. The longer she could keep him out of there, the better. Maybe by agreeing to go, she could stall him for a while.

"Okay, I'll go," she said, adding *but not anytime soon* silently to herself.

Brodie looked delighted. "As soon as my equipment arrives, then?" Darrell nodded reluctantly.

Darrell finished her meal quickly and headed back to the studio. The sky had darkened and rain pattered against the windows. She found Arthur Gill looking over her day's work, with Myrtle Tooth at his side.

Arthur Gill looked up at Darrell in amazement. "You must have been working on this all day!" Darrell nodded, pleased that he recognized her efforts.

He gestured at the painting and then turned to Myrtle Tooth. "I just had to show you this delightful piece. See how she has managed to capture the strange mixture of light and shadow on the narrow streets?" He turned back to Darrell. "The detail of the cobblestones and the roofs of the old cottages ... Remarkable!"

Myrtle Tooth smiled at Darrell and then turned, her clear green eyes taking in the painting. "Perhaps some of the history lessons have served to inspire your work, Darrell."

"If so," rhapsodized Arthur Gill, "they must have been fascinating lessons, Professor Tooth. Darrell has captured some amazing detail. Look how she has caught the light within this old French village. It is nothing short of astounding!"

Myrtle Tooth placed her had warmly on Darrell's shoulder. "I agree, it is certainly a fine day's work." She headed toward the door. "But to my eye, it holds more of a Scottish flavour than French."

"Do you think so?' questioned Mr. Gill, as he followed her out into the hallway.

Darrell stared blankly at the door that closed quietly behind the two teachers. Shaking her head, she gathered up her things and carefully covered her painting before heading upstairs to her room.

She looked at her bed and tried to think of everything that had happened since she had last crawled out of it. Her mind refused to comply, and after taking off her prosthesis she was asleep as soon as her head hit the pillow.

She dreamed of Luke.

CHAPTER NINE

Darrell spent every day of the following two weeks riddled with anxiety. She watched the summer storms that had swept in batter the school with cool rain and a wind that felt like it belonged more to the fall. The days were spent struggling with her self-portrait, her thoughts alternately drawn to and repelled by the cave on the beach. Her nights were filled with images of thundering horses and baby Rose being torn from her mother's arms by soldiers. One morning in late August when the dawn broke cloudy but not awash in rain, Brodie knocked on Darrell's door at seven o'clock. He stood at the door, beaming, with a full backpack tossed over his shoulder. Caught so early in the morning, Darrell didn't have time to come up with any kind of an excuse. Lily was still sleeping, so Darrell and Kate followed Brodie down to the garden. At the thought of returning to the cave, Darrell's mouth went dry and she fiddled absently with the mints in her pocket and stuck the charcoal pencil she had been using behind her ear. Kate complained bitterly as she trailed behind.

"I'm only coming because my laptop battery needs a recharge." Kate wrapped her windbreaker more tightly around her. "If it was running, I would totally refuse. But it's probably going to take least another hour, so I guess I'll come." She cast a skeptical eye at the windswept beach. "You're sure it's dry in this cave of yours? And anyway, you know we're supposed to keep in sight of the school. If we go inside this cave, we won't be able to see the school at all."

"Come on, you nit." Brodie grinned. "It's all for the sake of good science. Mr. Neuron would be proud of us, spending time outside of school *furthering our knowledge,* as he would say."

They set off through the grey morning light. It was not raining, but the sky was very low and the fog lay out on the surface of the water like a puffy white duvet.

Kate laughed as Darrell scrambled up the arbutus. "Like even Connie would be up at this hour of the morning," she scoffed. "Let's go find your cave and get it over with."

The coast deserted, they hurried down the winding path to the beach. Delaney ran up to join them as they came up to the rock wall.

"It's dark in there all the time," said Brodie as they walked, "so I've got some stuff we might need." His heavy-looking backpack was draped with all kinds of equipment that Darrell could not identify. He had also brought a couple of headlamps, and he handed one to Darrell.

"That's a funny looking flashlight," she remarked. "Why is it on a long strap like that?"

Brodie laughed and showed her how to strap the lamp to her head.

"It keeps your hands free while you're spelunking."

"While I'm … what?" Darrell asked in surprise.

"Exploring a cave. You can get more done if you're not holding a flashlight."

"Oh, yeah. Okay. Right." Darrell slid the small flashlight she had brought into the pocket of her jeans.

Brodie had to take off his backpack to squeeze through the crevice. Darrell handed the pack through to Brodie and followed Kate inside. The light creeping in from outside was so dim that they both immediately switched on their headlamps.

Kate gasped as they squeezed through the crevice in the rock, her scowl replaced by a look of awe. "This place is incredible!" They shone their flashlights off the walls as they looked around. "I don't know … Brodie, if you weren't such a fossil geek, we could be spending our time doing something fun instead of hanging out inside this cold cave," she teased.

Darrell smiled to herself. She suspected Kate might really be interested after all.

"Who're you calling a geek, tech head?" Brodie shot back. "At least we're outside, getting some fresh air, instead of stuck in front of a screen somewhere, surfing the net for computer games."

Kate laughed. "This place *is* pretty cool, actually. I'm glad you brought me."

"Oh no!" Darrell closed her eyes.

Brodie was by her side in an instant. "What's wrong?"

"This flash on my head is making me really dizzy. Every time I move, the light flicks and wavers."

Brodie laughed, relieved. "I thought there was something really wrong. It's okay. If it bugs you, turn it off. I'm used to wearing one and I can keep my head pretty steady. Until it gets really dark, you can follow mine."

"I'll wear it," said Kate. Brodie helped her strap it on, and Darrell pulled the flashlight back out of her pocket. Brodie shouldered his pack, and they set off slowly deeper into the cave. The last time she had been here, Darrell she had been alone, and surrounded by complete darkness. With her friends beside her and no fear of pursuit, the trip to the back of the cave seemed to take no time at all.

As they walked, Brodie told them something of the strange underworld they could see with the erratic bounce of light.

"Caves are usually formed by the work of water over thousands of years. A few are the result of earthquakes, and some are formed as a result of lava pushing to the surface from deep underground. This cave is so straight and true," he said thoughtfully. "It doesn't really seem like just a fissure in the rock or an area eroded by water. It reminds me of a lava tube. I'll have to check that out," he muttered to himself.

Kate interrupted his reverie. "We need you to do more than just talk to yourself, Brodie," she said, her tone sharp with anxiety. "You're the expert here." She looked around with some trepidation and touched the rock wall of the cave gingerly. "Is it safe to walk down through this cave? What if there's an — earthquake, or something?"

Brodie laughed. "We would be in just as much trouble above the ground in this area of the world if there was an earthquake, Kate."

Darrell frowned. "That doesn't really reassure me, Brodie."

"Or me," piped in Kate.

He smiled and shook his head. "Well, don't think of it too much then," he said. "Life is full of surprises.

Let's just hope that an earthquake doesn't choose now to hit this part of the coast, okay?"

The inside of the cave was starting to feel familiar to Darrell, and she noticed the rock outcropping where she had hidden her backpack on the day of her fateful voyage. Delaney led the way as the walls opened up near the rear of the cave. Brodie shone his headlamp around so that they could have a good look at the place, and Darrell tried to increase the illumination by adding the beam of her own light.

Kate looked around with wide eyes. The glint of minerals shone out as the light from the headlamps bounced off the rock surfaces. She reached up to run her fingers along the cave wall. "This really is something else. Thanks for bringing me in to see it."

"Wait 'til you see the stars of the show," Brodie remarked, and he began to look for the symbols on the wall with his headlamp.

Delaney's tail wagged a black shadow that rose right to the ceiling of the cave, which had taken on a whole new character with the light of Darrell's flashlight. Most of the way it followed a rough run straight down into the rock, but near the end it widened out into an area that could have been a large anteroom. The ceiling of the cave suddenly lifted high above Darrell's head and she could hear the distant sound of dripping water. Images swirled in Darrell's mind from the last time she had been in this place. The sick worry she felt about Luke and his family returned and lodged firmly in the pit of her stomach.

Brodie gave a low whistle, and the girls walked over to his side. He had found the symbols on the wall and was examining them closely with his light. Two symbols glowed a dull red in the wavering light, beside another, tree-shaped, which could just be made out as a soot-blackened smudge. Darrell brought her flashlight closer to the smudge, and in the more direct light, the shape of a tree appeared out of the dark. It was rimmed with the faintest trace of red, like a line of old blood, delineating the sooty symbol from the rocks behind.

Darrell peered at the symbols through the erratic light of their lamps.

"What do you think they mean, Brodie?"

Brodie looked puzzled. "I've never seen anything like these symbols before," he said slowly. "They're clearly extremely old, and drawn in a really primitive fashion, but ..."

"But what?"

He looked at her and shrugged. The light from his headlamp careened around the walls of the cave. "Usually cave paintings take the form of animals, or hunters. They were a means to record success and failure before people could really write. They were the first way history was written or drawn for people to remember. When I looked at these before," he continued, "I could see right away they were *not* cave paintings. They just don't look like anything I've ever seen painted by the indigenous people of this coast. That's why I think they're glyphs or runes."

"What do you mean? Is there any difference?"

"They're kind of similar, actually. Runes were sort of a rudimentary alphabet used by early Anglo-Saxon and Scandinavian people. Often they're used to symbolize the occult these days. Y'know, hex signs and that sort of thing. Glyphs are like hieroglyphics, the sort of picture story symbol that the Egyptians used."

He looked closely at the symbols, his nose almost touching the red pigment. Kate's jaw dropped as she looked at the symbols, and she exchanged a glance with Brodie.

Kate found her voice first. "What *is* this place?"

"I just don't know. These things look like a cross between glyphs and runes, but not like any cave painting I've ever seen a picture of. And look at this." He gestured to the symbol on the end that resembled a tree.

"What is it?"

"It's a different colour than the rest of them. The other two are reddish, like they were painted on with ochre, which was a common substance used in cave paintings. They're in the shape of a sword and a face or a mask of some kind. But this one shaped like a tree seems to be made of charcoal or something. It's really hard to see on the rocks in the dark. It looks like it's been burnt on with a brand, but of course that would be impossible. It's weird, but last time I was here I remember this tree looking much redder. I could see it more clearly on the wall, anyway. The charcoal was singed around the edges but the tree itself was the same ochre colour as these other glyphs." His voice trailed off.

Darrell looked closely at the symbol. She could see it was in the shape of a tree, but it was completely blackened and very difficult to see against the dark cave wall. With a ghost of remembered nausea, she thought about the glowing tree symbol in the cave near Mallaig and about how she had watched the glyph she looked upon now fade from glowing red to black, like a fire burning to ash when she returned from the past. She instinctively stepped away from the wall, hands tightly clasped behind her back. Could these symbols be the key to a doorway to the past?

Suddenly Brodie turned and grabbed something out of his pack.

"What are you doing?" Darrell cried.

Brodie looked determined. "I'm going to take a sample of both these substances." At Darrell's shocked look he said, "Don't worry, it'll be so tiny no one will ever notice. I'll be careful not to harm the symbols in any way."

"NO!" Darrell's voice rang out through the cave. "Don't touch them, Brodie." She began to babble. "I can't explain why but it's really important ... just ... just don't touch them." She frowned and muttered to herself. "I need to think about this for a while. I don't know what to do!"

Brodie gave Darrell a puzzled look and then turned back to the symbols. He reached up with a tiny scalpel-like instrument that he had pulled out of his pack.

"Don't worry, Darrell," Brodie said quietly. "I'm very careful and I take things like this very seriously. I wouldn't do anything to hurt the glyphs."

Darrell shook her head in disbelief. Brodie stood, unharmed, in front of her.

"Are you ready to go back to the school?' he said with a grin.

"I am," answered Kate, and turned to leave.

Darrell was baffled. Brodie had touched the symbols on the wall. Delaney was curled up on the floor of the cave near where she herself had fallen. If her time travel experience had really happened under these same circumstances, why was Brodie still standing above her and grinning? Her mind reeled with unanswered questions.

Darrell rose to her feet and stood in silence for a moment, staring at the symbols in the wavering light.

Kate stepped over beside Darrell and gently traced the outline of the second symbol: the shape of a knife or a sword. She turned and looked at the others, with her hand resting lightly on the rock face. Her eyes were huge in the lamplight. "I've never seen anything like these glyphs … or symbols …or whatever you call them. You've found something really important here, Brodie."

Brodie leaned forward for a closer look himself, his hand on Kate's shoulder.

"What do you make of *this?*" he said, excitement in his voice. As Darrell bent forward to look more closely, several things happened at once. Delaney stepped between Darrell's legs and she nearly fell. Darrell grabbed Delaney by the collar and clutched at Kate's shirt to break her fall. Kate teetered and bumped heads with Brodie, causing both headlamps to go out.

"Hold on, guys," breathed Darrell. "I think …." There was a loud bang, a snap, and then silence. The earthen room was dark again, and empty. Brodie's backpack slowly tipped over and settled itself on the sand.

CHAPTER TEN

Darrell lay on her back in the sand, feeling like she had just been through a tornado. Unlike the previous journey, which had taken place entirely in darkness, this time she opened her eyes to a dimly lit cave. She watched the colour slowly fade from a glyph on the wall. It was charred around the edges, in the shape of a sword, but still held a reddish glow. A river of emotion rushed through her. It had happened again … somehow. But this time, she was not alone.

She turned her head and gazed over at Brodie and Kate, lying flat on their backs in the sand. They both looked pale and unconscious. Darrell felt a sharp knife of fear slice through her stomach. She had learned from past experience not to try to move too quickly, but she was determined to find out the condition of her friends. As she rolled over onto her side and lifted her head, she saw with relief that Brodie was blinking, his eyes unfocused and bleary.

Darrell stood up. She staggered over to the other two and dropped to her knees between them. A heavy woollen skirt of rich purple billowed out around her legs. She ran her hands over the fine texture of the cloth, but nausea gripped her again. Rummaging in her pocket, she brought out a handful of unwrapped candy. She raised her eyebrows at the sight of it and examined it carefully, then popped one in her mouth. She thought for a moment about Luke's aunt, and shivered. Brodie groaned and she put a mint into his hand.

"Here, Brodie" she said. "Take this and put it in your mouth. I think it should make you feel better a little sooner." Brodie groaned again, but he did as Darrell instructed. Within a few moments, he was struggling to sit up. The two looked anxiously at Kate. The short red hair framed her face, and her freckles stood out clearly against her pale skin.

"She hasn't even opened her eyes yet," said Darrell, with worry in her voice. Brodie turned his head to look quizzically at Darrell's strange appearance, and opened his mouth as if to speak. Darrell looked back at him bleakly. Brodie seemed to make up his mind and closed his mouth abruptly. He crawled across the cave floor to Kate and peered at her through the strange red glow that lit the cave.

"She's coming around now," he said, relief on his face. "Just give me a mint. I'll slip it in her mouth and maybe it will make her feel a bit better. It seemed to help me." He took a small peppermint from Darrell's hand and pushed it between Kate's lips. She gagged and started to cough.

"That's just great, Brodie. Now she's going to choke to death." Darrell rolled her over onto her side and patted Kate on the back. Kate caught her breath and then opened her eyes wide.

"What's going on? Why do I feel so sick? Hey …" she gasped and choked again on her mint. She coughed violently for several minutes while Brodie and Darrell pounded her on the back. When she finally got her breath, she was able to finish her thought.

"LOOK AT YOU TWO!" she shrieked. Glancing down, she added, "LOOK AT ME!"

Darrell glanced over at Brodie and saw he was wearing a crude shirt made out of wool over a dirty under-shirt of some softer material. He wore rough trousers that only came to just below his knees. His shoes, like the one she had on her earlier journey, had wooden bottoms and leather uppers, and were ripped and worn. Darrell was surprised to see that her style of dress had substantially changed from the previous visit. She wore a long dress and over-skirt and a fine wool shawl. Kate's outfit mirrored Darrell's, but her skirt was made of a coarser cloth and she had a rough wool sweater for warmth instead of the shawl.

"Keep your voice down, Kate," whispered Darrell. "Do you want anyone to hear us before we figure out what we're doing?"

Brodie sat back on his heels and ran his hand across the stone wall. "It feels real," he muttered, "but it's not the same rock." He scraped the rock with his fingernail. "Definitely limestone. Not anything like the granite cave near the school."

"Brodie!" said Kate, furiously. "What are you mumbling about? Who cares what rock the cave is made of? This is serious!"

Darrell shook her head as if to clear it and looked at Brodie and Kate in wry disbelief. Now that she could see that Kate and Brodie were both okay, she felt seized with a sense of exultation. *They'll have to believe me now!* she thought triumphantly.

"What are you grinning at?" Kate crawled on her hands and knees across the sand and thrust her nose into Darrell's face. Kate's skin had gone from pale to bright red with remarkable speed. She looked as though she didn't know whether to hit Darrell or cry. Her wool skirt was rucked up around her knees, and her face reflected complete confusion.

Darrell's insides felt clenched. Her relief at being proved right washed away at the sight of Kate's misery.

"Look," she said, "I don't know what happened back there. I didn't intend for you guys to end up here with me." She shrugged and looked around. "I didn't intend to end up here myself ..." Her voice trailed off and she looked up at Brodie, still standing by the glowing glyph on the wall of the cave. It was becoming harder to see as the blood red light began to recede.

"You're right, Brodie. This is not our cave by the school. The problem is, when that glyph fades away, we are going to be in pitch darkness. We need to get closer to the mouth of the cave before we can decide what we're going to do."

"Darrell," Kate's voice was filled with fear, "if you have some idea of what is going on here, I want to hear about it *right now!*"

Darrell stood up and realized with a sigh that she had to balance again on a wooden peg instead of her prosthesis. She reached down and grabbed Kate by the hand. "I'll tell you all about it when we get a bit closer to the entrance, okay? C'mon. I know the way." She nodded her head at Brodie. "Better grab his hand, Kate. We need to stick together."

The last of the red light faded back into the rock like a candle puffed out, and Kate gave a little cry of despair. "What are we going to do, Darrell?"

Darrell clenched her teeth and reached out to touch the face of the rock wall in the dark. The rock was chill and a little damp under her fingers. She squeezed Kate's hand. "It's going to be okay. Let's just get to where the light's a bit better, then we'll figure out what to do."

Darrell led the way toward the mouth of the cave, her left hand tightly clenched by Kate. Her right traced their way along the cave wall, to avoid scrapes from the broken old barnacles that lined the rock surfaces. After a few long moments, she could see the glow of the entrance in the distance, and she sighed to herself with relief. Soon the three were seated on the damp sandy floor near the mouth of the cave, looking curiously at the strange clothes they were wearing.

Darrell rubbed the crease between her eyebrows and sighed.

"I'm … I'm not sure what happened back there …" she began.

Kate's lips began to tremble and her eyes filled with tears. She looked pleadingly from Darrell to Brodie. "This can't be happening. Please tell me this is something you've cooked up just to tease me, Darrell."

"Kate, try to stay calm." Darrell looked from Kate to Brodie. "This is a bit of a long story," she whispered, "but I'll try to give you the short version." She picked up a broken fragment of shell from the cave floor, took a deep breath, and began. In a rush of words, she told them about her discovery of the cave and about the strange series of experiences that followed. As she talked, of Luke and his mother, of the journey and the plague, she kept her eyes downcast so as not to see the disbelief she knew would be on their faces. She related as much as she could remember of the strange and remarkable journey she had taken. "And that's why I didn't want you to touch the symbols, Brodie."

Darrell paused and somehow found the courage to look up at her friends. "I know how I would feel if someone had told me a crazy story like this," she said evenly. "The truth is, I thought I was crazy, too, or maybe I just had a bad dream or something. But seeing the black tree glyph today has made things a bit clearer to me."

"Why's that?" said Brodie, with a tremor in his voice.

"Because that tree represents the mystical rowan tree in Arisaig that Luke told me about," Darrell replied. "And where we are now proves it. Somehow that glyph on the wall has pulled us all back in time."

Kate clutched Darrell's arms, her face a palette of emotions as she stared wildly from Darrell's eyes to the strange clothes they all wore. After a moment, she curled into a ball on the sand, tucked her face into the folds of her voluminous skirt, and sobbed.

Brodie knelt beside her on the cave floor and patted her back awkwardly. "It's going to be okay, Katie. Try not to cry." He looked at Darrell sharply as he struggled to find the right words. "Think about your tae kwon do training, Kate. You told me your instructor taught you to concentrate only on what's in front of you and to hold your opponent in the highest respect. Just think of this situation as a really tough opponent."

Kate lifted her tear-stained face out of her hands. Brodie pulled a linen rag from his pocket. He gave it a strange look and then handed it to Kate. She wiped her eyes and nose and tried to hand it back.

"You keep it," Brodie said hastily. "It used to be a Kleenex tissue, and I wouldn't have wanted that back, either."

"Just a minute," said Darrell, slowly. "Look at this." She pulled something out from behind her ear. It was a long thin piece of black material, hard with rounded edges.

"What's that?" said Kate in a troubled voice.

"It's charcoal," said Darrell. "But what's more important is what it's *not*."

"Okay, Darrell, now you've really lost me," said Kate, her face red from crying. "This is so weird! First we go through some kind of whirlwind storm, and we're all knocked out cold. Then, when we finally recover from that, all these strange things have happened to our clothes and our possessions ... and you!" She turned in fury to Darrell. "You brought us here. You need to get us back!"

"Wait a minute, Kate," Darrell said. "Stay with me a minute, here. When I said it's more important what this thing is not ... I meant it. When we went into the cave, I had a few things in my pockets. I brought a package of breath mints, and I stuck a pencil behind my ear. And this is what I have now."

They all looked down at the black object. It was the same length as a pencil and roughly the same diameter, but there any resemblance ended. Kate snatched the object up out of Darrell's hand. She turned round to the rock wall and began to rub it along a flat portion of the rough surface. It left dark, unmistakable marks. Darrell cleared her throat.

"I think it *is* a pencil, Kate. It's a pencil from before there were such things. This looks like the charcoal I sketch with, sometimes. I think it's what pencils looked like at this time … *when*ever we are."

Brodie looked at Darrell. "Your breath mints look more like old-fashioned peppermint candy. And what *was* my tissue seems to be an old piece of rag."

Darrell nodded. "And then there's this." She pulled up the hem of her skirt and showed them the wooden peg that replaced the elaborate prosthesis she had been wearing moments before.

More than anything, this sight seemed to have the largest impact on Brodie and Kate.

Kate looked at Darrell, aghast. "How are you going to walk on that thing?"

Darrell shrugged. "I did it the last time. It just takes a little practice and it hurts a bit more to walk." She paused and smiled ruefully at Brodie. "It also means I won't be winning too many foot races with you."

Brodie laughed, but looking at Kate's tear-stained face, he sobered quickly. He stood up and walked to the wall of the cave. "We have to decide what to do now." He turned to Darrell. "I know all about caves and fossils, but I have no experience with whatever's happened here. You're the expert now, Darrell. What do we do next?"

Both sets of eyes turned in the grey light toward Darrell. She swallowed. The magnitude of what had happened hit her like a blow. She had brought her friends through some kind of hole in the fabric of time. Whether she meant to or not didn't matter. They were here. Now what was she going to do?

The sound of a bark startled them and they all jumped. In the dim light of the cave, a dog ran in with something in his mouth. He dashed up to the group, spun in a tight circle, and dropped what he was carrying. He began licking Darrell's face.

"Delaney! Am I ever glad to see you! Good boy. Lie down." The dog lay obediently at Darrell's feet. He wriggled in place and put his head down on his paws, content. Brodie shook his head.

"Ah — Darrell, that's not Delaney. Delaney is a golden retriever. This dog, well — I don't have a clue *what* this dog is. Maybe he's a really dirty Lab. But he's not Delaney."

Darrell ruffled the dog's fur. "I'm sorry, Brodie, but you're wrong. When I went by myself through the cave the first time, Delaney was with me. When I got to this cave, I realized he looked different ... but inside, he was the same dog. He belonged to Luke's aunt from Arisaig. But he's still Delaney. Watch this."

She turned to Delaney and showed how he would sit, roll over, and shake a paw just as she had taught him over the summer. Finally, she gave him one of the peppermints to sniff and held her hands behind her back. She brought her two closed fists in front of Delaney and he gravely placed his paw on her right hand. She opened her palm and he licked the candy once before lying down in the sand, tail wagging gently.

"Dara! Are ye in here, lass?" A voiced echoed through the grey cave. The colour completely drained out of Kate's face. Brodie put a finger to his lips. Too late, Darrell reached to place a warning hand on Delaney's head. He barked joyfully and sat up.

The voice came again. It sounded relieved. "God be praised!"

The sound of armour echoed off the walls of the cave. Delaney jumped to his feet and ran to the figure who strode inside.

Darrell looked at Brodie and Kate, who stared back at her mutely. "It will be all right," she whispered and turned to the man who had joined them. She stiffened, and her stomach clenched at the sight of a uniformed soldier in the cave.

"Praise be to God," he said. "When the dog appeared again, I knew he must be bringing ye safely back to us."

Suddenly, Darrell recognized the soldier, and relief flooded through her.

"Luke!" she cried, and threw her arms around him. "You're all right! I thought you were one of the soldiers who chased me ..."

His blue eyes gleamed. "I am a soldier of the Laird's personal guard, Dara. Much has happened in the year since I have last seen ye."

Darrell gaped. A year! She did some rapid calculations in her mind, but came up blank. Time seemed to have a strange way of compressing here in the past. It had been two weeks since she had returned to Eagle Glen from her visit with Luke. Enough time for at least a year to have passed here in the fourteenth century.

Darrell felt a surge of panic. "How are Maggie and Rose? What has happened to them?"

Luke smiled sadly. "They are alive, but ..."

From the shadows of the cave came the sound of a muffled gasp. In one smooth motion, Luke pushed Darrell behind him and drew the small sword he wore in his belt.

"What is yer business here?" he spat.

Darrell stepped forward with a grin and squeezed his arm. "It's all right, Luke. I ... I have brought two friends to meet you this time."

Luke looked in confusion at Darrell. "I'm ... terribly sorry," he said. He pulled his back ramrod straight and turned to face Brodie and Kate as they stepped out of the shadows. "I offer ye my most profound apologies."

Kate's mouth hung open slightly and she appeared unable to speak.

"No offence taken," Brodie said quietly.

Darrell spoke up again. "I want to hear everything that has happened, Luke, every detail. But first you must meet my friends. Brodie and Kate, this is Luke."

Brodie put his arm around Kate's shoulders and steered her forward. He nodded toward Luke and even managed a nervous smile when Luke sheathed his sword.

Brodie turned to Darrell. "Darrell ... uh ... Dara ... what do we do now?"

Darrell smiled at Brodie but turned to Luke. "My friends and I have travelled a very long time to meet you, Luke. We are very tired and need to get our bearings. Is there a safe place for us to stay unseen for a little while?"

Luke looked troubled. "I was at the end of my watch, and I ... ah ... thought I would have a look along the beach. It was then that I saw Aileen's dog. I knew ye would be close by. I followed him straight to yer hiding place, and so I have made no preparations for ye to stay, as yet. But my mother will be so happy to see ye! I'm sure we can find a place for ye to stay in the castle ..."

"Luke ... uh ... I don't have time to explain now, but let's just say that we have been shipwrecked here, and we are seeking sanctuary with you from the plague."

Luke looked puzzled. "I do not see the remains of a ship ..." he began, but was interrupted by a shout. Darrell watched a horse thunder up the beach.

"Luke! There ye are! Our watch is over, we must return to the castle." The soldier looked down with some curiosity at Darrell.

Luke stiffened a little. "Angus. I have just discovered three victims of a shipwreck, washed up on our shore as they were heading to the north. They seek sanctuary within the walls of Ainslie Castle."

The other soldier looked discomfited. He turned his back to Darrell and whispered loudly, "I do not know how Hamish will take the news of strangers, Luke."

Luke frowned. "I serve Sir William and no other, Angus, and he would be the first to welcome stranded travellers into his home."

"But Sir William is gone, and probably dead from the plague on some distant shore." He looked nervously at Luke. "Hamish is captain of the guard," he insisted.

"Ye mustn't heed the chatter in the servant's hall, Angus. I have faith in Sir William yet," said Luke with a wry grin.

Darrell watched the soldier scratch his head and then several other places on his body. "All right," he said finally. "But we must report them immediately to Hamish. He is the captain and it should be his decision."

"Agreed." Luke turned to Darrell. "Miss," he said, with exaggerated formality, "we have a wagon on the lane above the beach, as we are escorting the lady of the castle on an outing. We can give ye a ride, if ye'd like."

Darrell smiled. "That would be most excellent, sir. We accept your kind offer." She watched as the two soldiers rode up the beach and the grassy bank near the stone steps that she remembered so clearly from her last visit. She twirled on her heel and re-entered the cave.

Once back inside, Darrell slipped over to kneel beside Kate and Brodie.

"Just follow along with me here," she whispered. "From the looks of our clothes, I think the best idea is to pretend you are my servants. We're going up to the castle. Luke is here, so I think things will be okay."

"Servants?" said Kate, her face incredulous. "What language is this that we're speaking? And how is it that I can understand a language I don't even know the name of?"

Darrell reached out and put a hand on the arm of both her friends.

In a whisper she said, "I'm not sure how it works, but it happened before when I went through the cave. We are speaking Scottish Gaelic. Did you see the plaid that the soldiers have wrapped around them?"

"They sure doesn't look like any kilts I've ever seen," whispered Brodie, "and my mother was born in Edinburgh!"

"Look," said Darrell, "it will make things easier if you can just accept that something we don't understand has happened here. Somehow we have ended up in the fourteenth century, and this is long before they made kilts that look like the ones we know today, believe me. Things happen for a reason. We must be meant to do something special here in this time. Whether it is to teach us something or to help someone else, I don't know. All I know is that we have to go now!" Darrell glanced over at a cleft in the rock near the cave opening. She rubbed at the crease on her forehead. "There's something different here," she muttered. "And it's more than just these new clothes. I just can't quite put my finger on it …" Shaking her head, she turned back to Brodie and Kate. "I think that we're safe for the moment, anyway. Just play along. We'll have a chance to talk soon." Limping slightly, she made her way out of the cave.

Brodie looked at Kate, and he gave her hand a quick squeeze. "Hang in there, Kate. We'll have you back to your computer screen in no time." Kate smiled back, tremulously. She knew that Brodie was sounding more confident than he felt. With a heavy heart, she followed him out into the bright sunlight.

CHAPTER ELEVEN

The brilliant sun seared their eyes after the dim cave, and it took a few moments before they could see the world into which they had journeyed. Shading his eyes from the sun, Brodie looked about in surprise. "Look at this place ..." he began. Kate clutched tightly at his arm, her lips pinched in a fearful line.

A rugged landscape surrounded them, with no sign of the heavily forested mountains they had left behind when they entered the cave near Eagle Glen. Instead, the land rose up in rocky fells covered with scrubby heather and low brush. A soft breeze that smelled of the sea gently blew their hair and cooled the heat that beat down from the dazzling sky.

Walking gingerly, Darrell led them along a sandy trail that ran up to a cart path on the hillside above the beach. Looking back, she could see the entrance to the cave was as well hidden as she remembered, blending into the rocky outcropping overlooking the water.

Luke was waiting at the foot of the stony pathway that rose up from the beach. He had dismounted from his horse and helped Darrell up the steps with a gallant air. At the top of the steps stood Angus, holding the reins of the two horses. Now that he was used to the idea of the shipwrecked strangers, he had begun to affect a heroic manner.

"These are lawless times and the plague has taken good men as well as bad. There are fewer now to guard the safety of travelers such as yerselves."

Darrell smiled to herself. "And we count ourselves lucky to have been rescued by so gallant a hero."

Angus blushed and turned to address Brodie. "Where is yer mistress's cloak, and the rest of her things?"

Darrell spoke up smoothly, though her face coloured. "We lost all in the shipwreck, good sir. The sea has stolen all we possess, except what we carry with us. Our — ah — cloaks went down with the ship."

A loud clatter precluded any further conversation as a carriage drawn by a pair of enormous black horses rolled up to the group and stopped. The horses were flecked with foam as though they had been running hard.

"Lady Eleanor, may I present the Lady Dara of ..." Angus turned in some confusion to Darrell.

"Of — of — Eagle Glen," she said, stumbling only slightly.

Lady Eleanor nodded, gently. "Angus tells me that ye have been shipwrecked," she said, her eyes shining. "How absolutely thrilling. I must hear all about it."

Angus helped Darrell enter the carriage and swung the door closed. She looked up in alarm.

"What about my frien — ah — servants? How are they to travel?"

Angus laughed. "Why, space will be found for them in the wagon that follows."

Darrell bit her lip and leaned out of the window to peek back at the wagon. "My servants are very precious to me. Will they be safe?"

"Of course. We are well-armed men who guard the Lady. Our journey is not far, and they will be delivered safe to ye once we reach Ainslie Castle."

Darrell craned out the window to watch as Kate and Brodie found themselves unceremoniously boosted up onto a prickly pile of hay on the rough cart behind. Delaney hopped up beside them and flopped down in the straw, tongue lolling. The soldier sitting on the rough board seat at the front clicked to the large brown workhorses who pulled the wagon. They set off along the path, slowly, with much creaking of wheels and bumping of ruts. The strong black horses set off again and the carriage pitched forward. Darrell's last glimpse of the cart behind was of two heads, one red, one dark, bobbing together in close conversation.

In the carriage with Darrell were Lady Eleanor and an older woman, whom Lady Eleanor introduced as her chaperone, Ernestina.

The carriage itself was made of wood and was little advanced in design over the cart in which Brodie and Kate rode. There were cushioned seats and a roof, but it still rolled on rough wooden wheels and jostled up and down with every rut in the road. Since the road was no more than a well-used cart path, there was not much opportunity for conversation, as the riders were too busy trying to hold on to take time to talk.

Darrell tried to get her bearings by staring out of the carriage window. She could see the village below, and she looked at it carefully. It was interesting to look down upon it from a new vantage point. The houses were tiny and had roofs that were made of a mixture of mud and hay. The spire of a church stood out like a beacon above all the small dwellings below. Several children chased a hoop they smacked along with a stick in the muddy, heavily rutted roads, and she watched one child herd a flock of geese. A few women stomped energetically at a washtub of clothes, keeping an eye on a group of toddlers nearby. Darrell just caught a snatch of song, borne on the wind as the women kept time with their stomping feet. In the distant fields beyond, she could see men at work, swinging scythes to reap early grain and using other strange, unfamiliar tools to break up the soil.

The small entourage rode on with the carriage only a few hundred feet ahead of the bouncing wagon. They rounded a corner, and Darrell saw that the track followed a ridge along a rocky coast. The water of the ocean was a brilliant azure until it dashed with snowy exuberance on the rocks below. The path began to drop, and Darrell saw the lines of a grey stone castle rise up, built on a cliff that overlooked the ocean. As they drew closer, she saw that the castle was on an island, connected to the land by a thin road that ran along a sandbar.

Darrell could feel the carriage surge as the horses hurried down the hill. Behind them, she could see Brodie and Kate bouncing on the back of the cart, as the work horses struggled to reach the island castle before the tide swept in. Luke and Angus rode at the rear of the group, keeping a careful watch on the vehicles as they approached the castle.

With splashing hooves, the horses pulled the carriage and the wagon up onto the small island. The water lapped over the sandbar behind them, and their connection to the mainland was temporarily lost to the tide. The castle that stood above them was breathtaking in size and grandeur. The walls that surrounded it were topped with a corbelled parapet patrolled by armed soldiers. A tall tower or keep stood at one end of the irregularly shaped courtyard and a number of other low stone buildings sprouted like mushrooms within the castle's walls. The carriage and cart thundered through the front entrance to the castle and pulled up to a halt.

High above, Darrell could see soldiers peering through the machicolations, the openings through which rocks or hot oil could be dropped on the heads of invaders attacking the castle, though there was no sign of oil or any other substance on the floor of the entranceway. For the moment, the only sound was the heavy breathing of the horses after their hard workout. Then Luke's horse clattered up and he leapt off. He swept open the door to the carriage and offered his hand to help Darrell get out.

"Welcome, my lady, to the Castle Ainslie, home of Clan MacKenzie."

As Darrell stepped down, the hem of her over-skirt snagged on the carriage and tore as she jerked it free. Lifting her skirts up more carefully, she made her way slowly along the cobbled surface to where Brodie and Kate were plucking the straw out of their clothes. They looked around open-mouthed at the inside of the castle.

"See to the horses," Lady Eleanor called to the boy who ran up to greet them. Angus slapped Brodie on the back and pushed him gently towards the stable boy. He turned to Darrell. "M'lady, yer servant here is a great strong fellow. He can help with the horses, with yer permission."

Darrell grinned at Brodie, who raised his eyebrows in alarm. "A fine plan, Angus," she said. "I will come down to collect you for the evening meal, Brodie."

Brodie scowled and, carrying a bridle and bit, trailed after the much smaller stable boy. Angus shook his head. "That servant of yers has a strange foreign look to him, m'lady. Is he a good worker, and dependable?"

Darrell laughed. "He is. And don't worry about his black frown, Angus. I would trust him with my life." *As he has trusted me with his*, she thought wryly.

Lady Eleanor spoke up. "He is welcome to join us in the Great Hall after he sees to the horses, or to eat in the kitchen, as ye wish, Lady Dara."

Kate scrambled over and stood close to Darrell, worried that she, too, would be sent on an errand. Darrell smiled at her reassuringly.

Lady Eleanor spoke up. "If ye are not too weary, Lady Dara, I will take ye on a tour of my home."

Darrell patted Kate encouragingly on the arm and, eyes wide open to the strange new world around them, they set off.

The entranceway into which they had driven was the main opening into the castle keep. At the moment of their arrival, it was a hive of activity. Stable hands and soldiers mixed with women hauling baskets filled with foodstuffs and clothing. Children ran through, chasing chickens and other livestock. The place had a rich, barn-like smell.

Darrell was relieved to find the ground was hard-packed clay, as it offered her some ease of walking. She noticed it was well swept, which, she thought to herself, was lucky, with the number of animals wandering through.

Eleanor pointed out the kitchen near the back of the castle walls, then she led Darrell and Kate up a tightly winding stone staircase to the next level. As Darrell climbed, her thoughts reached out to Luke and his family. What could have happened to them over the course of the past year? Little Rose must be walking by now, and what of Maggie? Luke had said they were safe, but ...

Darrell rubbed her forehead. She would have to find time to speak with Luke later. She was so filled with questions that she longed for her ragged notebook, sitting on her desk at Eagle Glen, just to help her organize the worries that tangled through her mind like the gnarled roots of Delaney's tree. She followed Kate out through a low stone archway and looked around. Most of the second floor was taken up by the Great Hall, which was a large open room with sconces on the walls to hold torches for light and rushes and straw strewn over the ground. The windows were made of glass within lead frames, and they opened to let in the daylight and fresh air.

"Our Ainslie Castle was built more than one hundred years ago," Eleanor told them, "but since my father has become Laird, he has made several changes. He brought in a glazier who made the glass for the windows. Now we have more than shutters to keep out the wind and snow."

She walked with them over to an enormous fireplace on one wall. "This new fireplace has meant the most change for us," she said. "Until last year, we burned our fires in the centre of the hall for all to keep warm." She pointed to a circular hearth that was bordered by stone and had clearly not been in use recently. "But now we have fireplaces throughout the castle, which keep us much warmer in our beds at night."

Kate looked at Darrell and raised her eyebrows. As Eleanor walked on ahead, Kate whispered, "Fireplaces, a new invention? How far back have we come?" Darrell shrugged. "I told you already. We're somewhere around the middle of the fourteenth century."

Kate closed her eyes and swayed a little on her feet. Darrell clutched her arm tightly. "It's going to be okay, Kate."

Kate's eyes flew open and her face reddened. "How do YOU know?" she said, miserably.

From the end of the hall, Eleanor turned around to look at them with impatience, and they scurried to catch up. In spite of the hurry, Darrell had to walk carefully because the floor was strewn with rushes and seemed slippery and sticky.

Eleanor sniffed. "The smell in here is terrible. It is time this hall was swept out and cleaned. It should have been done before our return."

"Why do you keep rushes on the floor?" asked Kate, without thinking. Eleanor looked at her out of the corner of her eye and pulled Darrell's arm out of Kate's grasp.

"The maidservant is quite ignorant of our ways," she whispered, "and speaks so forwardly, as though she were my equal."

Darrell laughed. "You must forgive her," she said teasingly, "for she comes from a far and distant place. Yet I am fond of her, and keep her to help me, all the same." Kate scowled at Darrell and didn't reply. Seizing the opportunity, Darrell patted Kate's shoulder and continued, "My Kate is so ignorant, I believe she does not know where we are, and I would venture to guess that she does not even know the date."

Eleanor took the bait, and looked suitably shocked. Then her natural kindness took over and she reached out to touch Kate's arm.

"It must be frightening to know so little, and yet ye are so loyal to yer Lady. This is the Castle Ainslie within the lordship of MacKenzie, and includes this land along with a group of small islands. It is the ancestral seat of the Clan MacKenzie, of which my father Sir William is the Laird. We are on the Western Highlands of Scotland." She turned to Darrell. "Do ye think it is necessary for me to tell her it is the year of our Lord 1351?" she asked seriously.

Darrell smiled. "No, I'm sure that is quite enough information for now."

Eleanor nodded. "Still, to be polite, I must answer her question about the rushes. They add warmth and softness to our floors, but they must be cleaned away periodically, for under them lay many crumbs and spills, and worse if the dogs have been up here."

Darrell and Kate made their way over the floor hurriedly.

Eleanor looked excited. "Ye must share my solar, as it is the nicest. I will have my room prepared, and yer things can be brought there." She looked crestfallen. "I had forgotten, all yer things have been lost." She looked critically at Darrell. "I am afraid ye are much too large to fit any of my clothes."

"Don't worry," said Darrell hastily. "I'll be just fine for now."

Eleanor nodded, and a number of women entered the hall and began erecting trestle tables and covering them with cloths. "Let me take ye both upstairs to prepare for the evening meal. I will have my maids bring ye water to clean and refresh yerselves after yer journey."

Eleanor bustled over to another spiral stone stair. Kate and Darrell exchanged a glance, then followed her upstairs to prepare for the evening to come.

The small staircase wound up from the Great Hall into Sir William's solar. It was vast room with a large curtained bed and a number of tables and chests scattered throughout. On the floor lay the skins of several animals, including two goats and a large brown bear.

"Where is her father?" whispered Kate, when Eleanor had hurried ahead.

"Last I heard, he was searching in the north for a place free of the plague," Darrell whispered back.

There were no hallways to be seen. Instead each room led into the next one, through one or more connecting doorways.

There was a heavy wooden door, which Eleanor moved to bypass. Darrell reached out and put a hand on her arm. "And this leads to …?" Darrell asked.

Upon entering the solar, Eleanor had removed the white wimple that had covered her face and neck in the carriage. Now she turned to Darrell with an embarrassed look and blushed to the roots of her pale blonde hair.

"It is the *garderobe*," she whispered, and made a move as if to keep walking past.

"The wardrobe?" questioned Kate, once again forgetting her role as humble servant.

Eleanor shot her an irritated look and took Darrell's arm, propelling her out of the anteroom and into another bedchamber.

Darrell still looked confused. "I'm sorry, but I am not familiar with that word. Is it another storage closet?"

Eleanor shook her head and stared at Darrell in surprise, clearly astounded by her new friend's ignorance. "It is the place where we empty the chamber pots, Lady Dara," Eleanor said with evident embarrassment. "The door is a heavy wood, so the smell will not travel through to the solar or other bed chambers." She bristled at Kate's amused smile and turned her back. "Tis the latest design, just installed two summers ago. The walls are a part of the buttress on this side and all the wastes drop into a channel that flows into the sea."

Kate looked disgusted. "You drop untreated sewage into the ocean?"

Darrell gave her a warning glance. "It sounds like a very efficient system," she said, steering Eleanor away from Kate.

She changed the subject. "Please show us your room." Kate had followed behind Darrell and Eleanor, tossing a last shocked glance over her shoulder at the primitive facilities.

Darrell looked around Eleanor's solar as they entered. She and Kate were sleeping here on straw pallets that were made up on the floor. Eleanor had two maids who normally slept in the room, but they were summarily sent down to sleep in the kitchen. The room was a large one on the uppermost floor. Darrell sat down on Eleanor's bed, which had a wooden frame and woven strips of leather supporting the feather mattress, with a cover made of fur. She watched as Eleanor pulled back and fastened the heavy linen hangings surrounding the bed. Eleanor laid her discarded wimple on a large chest meant for holding her clothes and sat on the window seat. She turned her back to a view that overlooked most of the island.

Darrell could see that Kate was as struck by the plainness of the room as she herself was, but she hastened to murmur appreciatively at the view. Two of Lady Eleanor's maids scurried into the room bearing small pitchers of lukewarm water and poured it into a bowl that sat on a tiny corner table.

After a quick wash in the basin, Eleanor insisted that Darrell remove her torn over-skirt. Darrell agreed and sat, secretly far more cool and comfortable in her light chemise and petticoat, gazing out the castle window. Eleanor pulled out her stitchery basket.

Kate sat beside Darrell on the cushioned window seat. "You should draw this view," she said with a tiny smile at Darrell's twitching fingers. Darrell smiled back, relieved to see that Kate's panic seemed to have calmed somewhat.

"Ye are an artist?" asked Eleanor. "Then ye must have materials!" She dropped her sewing basket and pressed a roll of parchment paper into Darrell's hands. "I have no use for the parchment," she said with some regret, "as I cannot draw and I have no one to send a letter to. The plague has made sending messages far too expensive and risky in these terrible times."

Darrell accepted the parchment and turned eagerly to the view from the high window, one piece of her charcoal streaking across the page. As Darrell drew, Eleanor returned to her stitchery basket and began to mend the tear in Darrell's over-skirt. She glanced up at Darrell and said shyly, "Forgive me my impertinence, Lady Dara, but can ye tell me why yer hair is uncovered and why ye walk on a stick of wood instead of a foot?"

Darrell thought quickly. She knew very few people would survive amputation in this day of primitive medicine. "I was born without a foot and have known no other way of walking," she said, her face colouring slightly. "And after the shipwreck, we were left with only the clothes we are wearing."

Lady Eleanor looked horrified. "Ye are lucky to have yer life after such a disaster!" She looked at Darrell with undisguised interest. "Still, if all ye have lost are yer possessions," she said kindly, "then the good God and yer servants have protected ye well." She glanced sideways at Darrell, appraisingly. "Yer size must have also protected ye. Ye and yer maid are the tallest girls I have ever seen!"

Darrell exchanged an amused glance with Kate and turned back to her drawing.

Eleanor seemed delighted with her new guests. Stitching carefully, she gossiped merrily about the various happenings in the castle and around her father's lands.

Darrell watched Eleanor's skill with a needle and thread with awe. "I could never sew as well as you," she remarked, wondering what Eleanor would think about sewing machines.

Eleanor smiled and bowed her head modestly. She gestured at the rough sketch Darrell held in her lap. "And I could never draw pictures as ye can, Lady Dara," she replied. "We each have our own skills given to us by God."

From her perch by the window, Kate snorted audibly. "Some of us have great skills in things other than stitchery or art," she said with disdain. "And we weren't *given* them at all. We *earned* them." Darrell grinned.

Eleanor, pointedly ignoring Kate, changed the subject and once again took up her stream of chatter.

Darrell, trying to keep the peace in the unexpected rivalry for her attention, only caught the end of one of Eleanor's remarks. "I'm sorry, what did you just say?"

"I said, I worry so much for my father. He has gone to visit our Nordic cousins to see if they are safe from the plague that ravages our land. He has warned me to no longer accept servant help from anywhere outside the castle ... even the village." She gazed pointedly at Kate, and then smiled ingratiatingly at Darrell. "Of course, in yer case we will make an exception. Tis only charitable to do so."

Kate rolled her eyes, and Darrell poked her gently with the end of her charcoal, willing her to silence. Kate smouldered but held her peace.

Eleanor, gazing out the window, blushed, and withdrew her head. "Tell me, Lady Dara, what do ye think of the captain of the guard?"

Darrell tried to keep any expression out of her voice. "The captain of the guard? I don't think I've met him."

Eleanor's face remained pink. She had mended the tear in Darrell's skirt with a series of tiny, fine stitches so that the repair was almost invisible. Darrell smiled appreciatively at the fine work and took it over to show Kate. She was enjoying Kate's role as maidservant and teased her by dropping the dress into her lap.

"Alas," Darrell said, dramatically, "if only your stitchery, young Kate, was as fine as that of Lady Eleanor ..."

Kate scowled. "I'll give you a few stitches, if you'd like, Darrell," she muttered under her breath. Eleanor looked disapprovingly at Kate and whispered to Darrell,

"M'lady, I think ye should seek a less sullen maidservant. I know many a fair young girl that would delight in the position."

Darrell laughed. "Oh, I think she'll do for now," she said, as Kate frowned her disapproval. Inwardly, Darrell heaved a sigh of relief. The subject of Hamish, Captain of the Guard, had clearly been dropped for now. She glanced sidelong at Eleanor, thinking. Why had she blushed at the mere mention of his name? A gong reverberated deep within the walls of the castle. Darrell filed away her thoughts of Eleanor and Hamish for another time, and the girls began to put away their things.

Dinner was a wonderful event, served with much merriment in the Great Hall. Darrell had sent Kate on a trip down to the stables in time to rescue Brodie and help get him cleaned up for the evening meal. The servants joined the family in the Great Hall to eat, so neither Kate nor Brodie were considered out of place. They sat together further down the long table from where Darrell was seated and drank in as much of their surroundings as they ate food. Delaney slunk under the diners' chairs and feasted on dropped scraps before creeping back and curling up under Darrell's chair.

The excitement of the celebration was marred for Darrell when Eleanor swept her over to introduce

Hamish, Captain of the Guard, just as dinner began. "Ye really must meet our new visitor, Hamish," Eleanor said.

Hamish bowed and kissed Darrell's hand, but he lifted his head to look up at her with a puzzled look in his eye. Darrell's stomach dropped and she quickly withdrew her hand and hurried to her place at the table to avoid any complicated questions. With vivid memories of a snarling Delaney, smoky torchlight, and a terrified run across the beach racing through her mind, she made a mental note to avoid him if at all possible. The last thing she wanted was to remind him of the events of their brief first acquaintance.

The meal was a feast in celebration of a local saint, and Darrell and her friends were welcomed with great ceremony. As ranking officer in Sir William's absence, Hamish began the evening with a toast. He presented a container of salt to Lady Eleanor, who responded with reddened cheeks and a beaming smile. Then a baker came in and cut the top off of a beautiful round loaf of bread. The upper crust was divided among the Laird's family and the guests, and the rest of the bread was sent further down the table for the other members of the household to enjoy.

Lady Eleanor played hostess to the introduction of a succession of delicious dishes. There were twelve courses in all, beginning with a fruit tart in pastry and including a tiny omelette, roasted salmon and chicken, and a selection of cakes and cheese.

Darrell made a concerted effort to avoid Hamish's gaze. She noted with some interest how he lavished attention upon Eleanor throughout the meal. Seated on her right, he ordered the servants brusquely to ensure that her plate and cup were never empty, and he spent much of the meal with his hand resting lightly on her arm.

Wanting to avoid Hamish's eye as much as possible, Darrell turned to Lady Eleanor's chaperone from the carriage, Ernestina. "Has this region been much affected by the plague? It seems there is much sorrow to be found in the village."

Ernestina nodded. "I, myself," she said piously, "take time out every day to pray at the Monastery of St. Columba of Iona, that I might help the people with God's holy strength. That is where Eleanor and I were today, when we came upon ye near the water." She rolled her eyes heavenward and rubbed the rosary she wore around her neck.

The couple sitting between Darrell and Kate stood up and strolled away. Darrell looked thoughtfully at the Ernestina for a moment and then turned in her own chair to listen to Kate and Brodie, now within earshot.

"I can't understand how these people can be so small when they eat so much food," whispered Kate to Brodie.

He grinned and swallowed a small cake from a platter in front of him. "Think of how you eat after you have been doing tae kwon do for an afternoon," he replied in a low voice. "These people have no labour-saving devices. They do everything from scratch and they have to work very hard." He started to tick things off on his fingers. "No cars, no phones, no water pipes, no washing machines, no computers ..."

"What is this '*computer*'?" interrupted a young girl sitting beside Kate who had been listening with growing puzzlement to Kate and Brodie's whispered conversation.

Brodie turned red and looked at Kate for help.

She grinned at the girl. "I'm sorry," she said sincerely, "he is just an ignorant boy who comes from a far and distant place. Still, I am fond of him, and I keep him around to help me, all the same." Kate looked at Darrell and they dissolved in giggles, while Brodie and the young girl gazed at them in great puzzlement.

Lady Eleanor went to bed soon after the evening meal, bringing the girls up with her. After making use of the garderobe to their great amusement, Darrell and Kate readied themselves for bed. Eleanor, attended by her maids, was rolled up in her covers and securely enclosed by the heavy linen hangings around her bed.

Once she was sure that Eleanor was safely tucked in bed out of earshot, Kate rolled over toward Darrell on her nearby pallet and they conducted a whispered conversation.

"Did you see the mess on the floor after the meal?" whispered Kate, disgust in her voice. "These people just throw their bones and scraps on the floor after they eat. It's awful."

Darrell smiled sleepily. "I think they were throwing the scraps to the dogs. I saw at least three dog fights over the course of the banquet."

"No wonder the Great Hall stunk so badly when we walked through it today." Kate punched the straw pallet she was lying on. "And I'm sure I saw one puppy pee in the corner by the door to the kitchens. At least Delaney's house trained."

Darrell smiled in spite of her sleepiness. "Make that *castle* trained."

"Do you think Brodie is okay? Where do you think he's sleeping?"

"I'm sure he's fine," replied Darrell, keeping her voice very low. "Since he's taken on the job of stable boy, I'm sure he must be down there with Delaney." She changed the subject. "I want to go back and have a peek at the cave again tomorrow. When Delaney came in, he had something in his mouth, but I didn't get a good look at it. I have a hunch it has something to do with why we are here."

"What do you mean?"

"I don't know, Kate. And I'm not really sure … just something about the cave was different from

193

when I saw it last. We left the cave in such a hurry that I didn't get enough time to properly look around. And I couldn't even get a good look back from the carriage ..."

"Right, I remember that," interrupted Kate, sarcastically. "*We* got to ride on the back of a creaking wagon filled with straw. My back is still killing me from the ruts. And I'm sure that Brodie is down in the stable right now, sneezing his head off as your loyal servant should. As I recall, *you* were riding in air-conditioned comfort in a padded coach."

Darrell snickered quietly. "Okay, okay, so the coach was better than the wagon. It was still pretty bumpy, y'know. And definitely not air-conditioned, except that there was no glass in the windows."

She paused. "Anyway, in the coach, I was thinking that this whole trip has to do with what we were learning from Professor Tooth this summer. Eleanor confirmed it this afternoon. We are smack in the middle of the European outbreak of the Black Plague."

Kate closed her eyes and leaned back on her bed. "I know that must be true," she whispered, "but I still find it so hard to believe." She looked at Darrell's face, lit by the flickering light of a small tallow candle, and her eyes filled with tears. "I really want to go home now, Darrell. There are so many things that have happened that I don't understand."

Darrell nodded and reached over to pat Kate's arm. "It will all work out, Kate. Somehow everything is tied into this cave. I'm sure by tomorrow we will be able to make it back to the school."

CHAPTER TWELVE

Darrell woke the next morning before dawn, feeling restless and worried. She was missing something, and she couldn't think what it could be. She got up and dressed quietly, cringing a bit when she touched the slightly sticky mints that were still in the pocket of her skirt. *I'll have to get rid of this mess somewhere,* she thought absently as she tiptoed downstairs to the stables. She could see the small stable boy at the end of the dark aisle carefully carrying an oil lamp. She put up her hand to hail him when she tripped and stumbled over something in the dark. She grabbed the low wall of one of the stalls and managed to keep her feet. Looking down, she saw Delaney, curled up like a brown apostrophe on the hay. He smiled up at her and held up his front paw, which had a small dirty bandage wrapped around it.

"Delaney," she said with dismay. "What happened to you?"

"He got his paw under Primrose's hoof, m'lady." The small stable boy had heard Darrell's clumsy entrance and come over to investigate. "I think the bone is broken," he added.

"Oh, Delaney!" She patted him gently on the head.

"I've left yer servant to sleep, miss," the stable boy whispered. "I tried to rouse him this morning but he just rolled over and would not get up."

Darrell smiled weakly, still worried about Delaney. "I do need to speak with him about the dog, so let's try a wet rag on his head. I'm sure that'll do the trick."

The stable boy sped off to get the water, giggling.

Darrell turned back to Delaney and found he was holding something in his mouth. She took it and stood up to peer at it in the gloomy lamplight.

A wool stocking, she thought. *Where have I seen this before?*

A voice behind her made her jump. Quickly, she jammed the stocking into her pocket before she turned around.

"Here's the water, m'lady." The stable boy grinned impishly.

"I'm sorry," Darrell muttered. "I've changed my mind. Let's let him sleep a while longer. I've just remembered something I have to do ..."

Ten minutes later, Darrell was scrambling down the road to the beach. The kitchen had been a flurry of activity as she ran out the door to the garden (*Just like Eagle Glen*, she thought with a pang) and she was sure that no one had noticed her departure. She had stopped on the way through the great hall to pick up an old hawthorn stick she had seen lying discarded in a corner.

Using the stick as a cane tremendously aided her progress, and by using a hop-step combination over the many ruts, she was able to almost run down the road to the town.

My leg must be getting used to this prosthesis, she thought sardonically.

In less than half an hour she made her way down the stone steps and onto the beach. As she limped down the final steps, Darrell heard a scratching sound behind her, and her heart jumped into her throat. She whipped around, only to find Delaney limping down the path behind her.

"Silly dog," she muttered quietly. "You should be home resting that sore paw of yours." She patted his head and stepped onto the beach. Slowing down to catch her breath, she watched Delaney snuffle off down the beach. She pulled the stocking out of her pocket and picked her way across the rocky shore to the entrance of the cave.

She didn't smell the smoke until she had actually stepped into the opening itself, and then it was too late.

A dry voice spoke behind her. "And who might ye be, lass?"

Darrell whirled around to face an old man, wildly bearded and wearing little more than rags.

Darrell's heart felt like it had frozen in her chest. Her feelings of unease had been justified.

"I ... I found this stocking at the castle," she said lamely. The man stared at her through blue eyes that looked strangely familiar. He nodded for her to continue.

Darrell groped for something to say, and then decided on the truth, or part of it. "I was here yesterday, and I saw the mate of this stocking tucked in the cave here. I ... I ... just came down to ... to satisfy my curiosity."

The old man looked at her calmly.

"Well, my dear," he said. "I'm afraid ye couldn't have chosen a worse time to be curious." He called into the cave. "Sir William, I believe we have a problem."

Darrell turned to see the entire doorway of the cave filled with the bulk of an enormous man wearing a uniform similar to that of the castle soldiers. He was wrapped in a swath of plaid, and the links of his mail clinked and rattled as he stepped out of the cave. He was as heavily bearded as the old man, but almost twice the size.

Darrell was speechless. In an age where she qualified as a large girl, this was surely a giant. And yet the voice, when he spoke, was gentle.

"I've never seen ye around Ainslie, my girl. I would've remembered that wee wooden foot, I'm sure. Are ye a friend to my daughter, then?"

Darrell swallowed. "I … we … my friends … ah … servants and I were shipwrecked on your beach," she stumbled. She took a deep breath and tried again. "The Lady Eleanor has welcomed us into Ainslie Castle, that we might find sanctuary from the Black Plague."

The giant roared with laughter. "My Ellie," he said with evident delight, "was probably so excited by yer adventures that she kept ye up all night." He sat down on a large boulder with a clank and turned to the old man. "As she's a friend of Ellie's, Iain, I guess we'll just have to leave her here in the cave until all the nonsense is over."

Darrell looked from one bearded face to the other with dawning understanding. She pointed her finger at the giant.

"You must be Sir William, Eleanor's father." She turned and looked at the old man. "And if I had to guess from the colour of your eyes, I would say you must have a son named Luke."

The old man grinned through his beard and spoke

to the giant. "She's a quick study, this one. Perhaps she can deliver us news from the castle ..."

He was interrupted by a shout, and Darrell looked up to see Luke careening down the road from the castle on his horse. The animal scrambled down the bank and then thundered up the beach to where they stood.

"Father ... Hamish is mounting his men!" he gasped, and slid off the horse. "I took the fastest horse, but they were but moments behind me."

Darrell grabbed Luke's arm. "Please tell me what's happening."

"Dara! There is no time! Ye must flee back to the castle. Take this dirk!" He pulled a slim knife from his stocking. A ray of sun crept over the horizon and gleamed on the blade of the knife. She heard a crash and looked up to see what seemed a river of mounted men, pouring down from the castle road onto the beach.

Leading the charge was Hamish, looking much more imposing atop his horse than on foot.

Darrell recognized several of the soldiers who rode beside him as those who had surrounded Luke and his family and frightened her on her first visit to this place.

Sir William put his hand on her shoulder and gently pushed her behind him. Darrell stepped back against the rocks, her hands behind her. Sir William looked up at Hamish, ignoring the other mounted soldiers. "Hail, young Hamish. Would this be a wee committee to welcome me home from my travels?"

Hamish quailed for a moment at the sight of the large man. He looked around at the troops mounted beside him and swallowed.

"Not quite, Sir William. Ye have been gone so long, we at Ainslie Castle had taken ye for lost."

"So I have heard from my shipmate's son, Hamish. He tells me that there may be other plans in play ... something to do with my daughter?"

Hamish shifted in his saddle. His tone was condescending. "Aye, yer spy has told ye well, Sir William. With ye dead and gone, and no male heir, it will fall to the Lady Eleanor to look after Ainslie Castle until she produces a son. I plan to marry her and help her with both projects."

Darrell remembered Eleanor's blushing face from the previous day, and Hamish's plans snapped into place in her mind so clearly they almost clicked. She shook her head. *I have to hand it to you, Hamish,* she thought. *You certainly don't think small.*

Sir William stood very still, but from her position behind him, Darrell watched his hands flex. "I'm afraid yer plans are spoiled then, lad," said the large man quietly. "For I have returned from my journey and plan to take my place at the head of the Laird's table."

Hamish sneered and gazed over the water. "Looks to be a terrible storm brewing ... dangerous waters out there. When the Laird's body is found washed up on shore, I don't think there will be much argument if the captain of the guard helps console the Lady Eleanor in her great loss." He returned his gaze to Sir William. "Look behind me, old man. Ye may have yer spy, but ye have been gone a long time. The loyalty of the castle guard now rests with their captain."

Luke stepped forward. "I am no spy, Hamish. It is ye who are the traitor against yer Laird." He raised his voice. "Who will stand with me, and fight for Sir William against this traitor?"

Hamish didn't even glance at the crowd of mounted men. He turned his gaze on Darrell.

"Don't think I have forgotten ye either, lassie." He grimaced as though a bad taste had crossed his tongue and gestured to one of the soldiers. "Jacob, that girl has been nothing but trouble. Seize her!"

"Not under my command!" Sir William's voice rose to a roar. "Who's with me?" He reached behind his shoulder and drew out an enormous broadsword. Luke jumped to his side and suddenly all the soldiers had blades in their hands. Sir William swung his sword at Hamish and the fight was on.

The air rang with blows as soldier turned against soldier. Several horses screamed, and Darrell, terrified, stepped backwards into the cave. From the relative safety of the cave, she watched the battle unfold outside. It was hard to tell who was winning, or even who was fighting for whom, as by this time all the men were hard at it, and the slash and clang of metal against metal was deafening. Her heart pounded and her head rang with the noise.

The handle of the knife was warm in her palm, and she shifted it uneasily from hand to hand. Darrell glimpsed a rock shelf near the cave entrance. In the dim light she could see a niche where the rock levelled out to form a ledge almost two metres above the ground. Perhaps she could hide the knife in there, as she most certainly could do nothing else with it. Peeking over, she could see the ledge was tucked in behind a dark face of rock. It held a threadbare roll of rough cloth and a few scraps of dried fish.

Suddenly a man leaped in the entrance and pushed past Darrell. She staggered back to see that it was Luke's father. He thrust his hand into the bundle and pulled out a short sword. Blood ran down one side of his face, but he was grinning.

"Been through too much to get back here to give up now," he said. "'Tis enough to make a man feel young again," he added and jumped back out the cave opening.

The battle outside seemed to be ebbing, judging from the noise. The clamour was dying down, with fewer ringing blows being struck. Darrell willed herself to be calm. She took a step toward the entrance to peek outside when she was thrust back against the wall of the cave by a small form.

"I thought ye might be in here, lass." Hamish grabbed Darrell by the arm.

She struggled to push him away. "I thought you were fighting your Laird?"

Hamish grinned and his teeth looked brown and broken in the dim light. "He went down in the first sortie, lassie." With strength that belied his size, he pinned her to the wall with one hand and pulled up one of his leggings. A broad white scar bloomed on the back of one calf. "I believe I have a score to settle with ye, miss."

He swung around and held his bloody sword to her throat.

Without a second's thought, Darrell slashed at the hand holding her arm with the slim blade that she still held. Hamish cried out and dropped her arm. Realizing she was free, she plunged deeper into the cave. A brown blur surged through the door and to Darrell's side, and together she and Delaney flew into the black recesses of the cave.

She could hear Hamish shout behind her, calling for a torch, but she ran on, blindly, in the dark. Guided only by the feel of the wall under her hand, which was raw from the rough surface, she fled into the darkness, Delaney at her heels.

Darrell's leg was in excruciating pain. The wooden peg, though bound tightly, had no flexibility and pounded brutally into her leg as she ran. A rock caught her foot and, unable to keep her balance, she felt herself falling. A memory of another fateful fall in another world rose up from deep within and told her to roll her head and legs in a ball. She hit the ground very hard, jarring one shoulder painfully, slid on the sand, and crashed against the rock wall of the cave.

Another shout echoed behind her, and she flailed in the dark, feeling Delaney at her side and trying to get up. As her right hand groped for purchase on the wall, she was flooded with a sudden realization. There was a vicious yank on her arm, and she was gone.

Chapter Thirteen

Her head was spinning, pounding, whirling. Darrell curled up into a ball and, eyes tightly closed, forced herself to breathe evenly. She slipped one of the mints from her pocket into her mouth. The spinning slowed, and as the hot, sweet taste of peppermint filled her mouth, the sick feeling in her stomach eased. She clasped her arms around her knees, almost weeping with relief. Apart from the sore leg and shoulder, this was definitely an improvement over the last trip. And she knew there would be at least one more trip to come. She swallowed.

Her friends were lost, behind more than a rock wall in a cave. They were stranded in time.

This sick thought propelled Darrell to her feet. Though her heart still pounded with fear, the lingering pain forced her to limp slowly to the entrance of the cave. Her leg was throbbing, although it was certainly easier to walk in her comfortable prosthesis than with a wooden peg strapped to her leg. Nauseated with fear and confusion, she sat down to take stock near the cave entrance, where evening light flooded in through the rock.

Looking around, she saw that for the first time after a journey there was no sign of Delaney. Still, she didn't have time to worry about him at present. The priority right now was to go back in time to find Brodie and Kate, and she knew she had to do so quickly. Every minute she was here meant much more time lost in the compressed world of the past.

Hurry ... hurry ... make a decision ...

This was crazy. She tried to stop her mind from whirling and to catch her breath.

This time I need to be better prepared, she thought grimly. Darrell scrambled to her feet and slipped through the crevice.

The run up the beach seemed to last forever, though the pain in her leg had started to slide to the back of her mind, edged out by the fear for Brodie and Kate that tore at her gut. Her mind gnawed at the problem — find Brodie and Kate, get them back to the cave. And what about Hamish?

The gravel crunched underfoot as at last she turned onto the winding path up the cliffs to the school. Her breath was coming in ragged gasps. She crept upstairs, anxious to avoid anyone, and grabbed a few essentials from her room. The seconds sped past as she applied an extra layer of padding and, fingers fumbling, re-adjusted her prosthesis snugly. She slipped down the corridor to a room near the stairs, having to hide in a doorway only once to avoid a student coming out of the bathroom. One item left.

Darrell peered through the door of the darkened library. When she saw that the place was deserted, she slipped inside and ran straight to the personal health section. Darrell read rapidly through the titles on the shelf and selected a book. There would be room for only one. Quietly, she stepped through the door of the small library, closed it behind her softly, and headed for the stairs.

"Darrell! There you are."

Darrell's heart sank into her boots. She turned around, slowly.

"Hi, Lily."

Lily came bounding up, talking a mile a minute. The only words Darrell could make out were "Conrad" and "police."

"Wait a minute, wait a minute, Lily. I'm in kind of a hurry. Could we talk later on?"

"NO, Darrell! I have to speak to you now."

Darrell sighed and glanced impatiently at her watch. Time had become her adversary and it seemed to be flying on wings of lightning. She rubbed her eyes and cut Lily off again.

"Stop a minute, Lily, will you? I am dealing with something here that is like life and death — no, really it's more important than life and death. I will listen to what you have to say, but I can only give you three minutes. I'm not kidding. THREE MINUTES! Now tell me the problem."

Lily shook her head. "Darrell, you are always so dramatic. Life and death, my foot." She blushed suddenly. "Oh, sorry, Darrell."

Darrell rolled her eyes. "Like I haven't heard *that* one before." She looked at her watch. "Two minutes," she said, threateningly.

"Okay, okay, I'll only take one. I just wanted to know if that Conrad Kennedy has been bothering you again lately."

"No," said Darrell, slowly. "Why?"

"Because it seems that every time I'm out for a swim in the bay, he's there, driving his boat up and down. He has nearly run over me a couple of times and I am ready to report him to the police."

"Did you tell your swim coach?"

"Yeah, and she's going to report him on Monday to the office. I just wondered if you wanted to add anything to the report."

Darrell thought about the white plastic boxes filled with CDs and computer parts. With Brodie and Kate gone, Conrad suddenly seemed a lot less important.

She started down the stairs. "I'll talk to you about it tomorrow," she promised Lily. *If there is a tomorrow,* she added, silently. "If you want information to give to the police, I'll be able to tell you some more about it then."

Lily stopped on the staircase and watched Darrell run down the hallway. "Okay, Darrell. I'll talk to you about it then." As Darrell sped down, she heard Lily's voice echoing, exasperated, down the stairwell. "For an artist, you sure don't sit still very often!"

Darrell checked her watch. It had been a little more than an hour since she had sat in the entrance to the cave. With the strange way that time seemed to compress in the past, who knew how long Brodie and Kate had been on their own at Ainslie Castle? Darrell groaned to herself. It could have been days. Her heart dropped into her shoes. *I hope I'll still have friends by the time I make it back,* she thought grimly.

Darrell crept down the back hall toward the garden. The door cracked open in the sooty night, and she slipped quickly through. Darkness had become her ally, and she wanted no eyes to follow her this night.

The sky was heavy and dark and the air was dense with humidity. In the garden, the air felt dead, and Darrell could smell a storm coming. The waves lapped the beach lazily, as though too thick and oily to travel with any conviction.

Against the obsidian sky, Darrell slipped down the path to the beach. The going was difficult, and she was forced to move more slowly than she wanted. When she finally felt the rocky surface change to sand, she began to run. She flew down the beach, avoiding the waterline and keeping to the hard packed sand. Once, she glanced behind as she ran towards the enormous boulders that marched down to meet the water. Was there a light, high up on the cliffs behind? It was extinguished so quickly she doubted her own eyes. She stopped to listen, and then continued her quick, cautious pace toward the rocks.

As she neared the shelter of the place where the cliffs met the sea, a tangle of voices rose up from the water near the boulders that lined the far side of the beach. The voices travelled, muffled through the damp air. Darrell started, then threw caution aside and ran blindly toward the rock wall. Reaching it, she clung for a moment to the rocky cliff face, trying to catch her breath. A stitch burned in her side, and in spite of the new padding she had applied, her leg was on fire.

She could see the boat clearly now, almost up onto the beach. What she could not see was who was on board. She hoped that the moonless night would shroud her presence from whoever was steering the vessel. Panting, she slipped inside the crevice and disappeared from sight.

Darkness wrapped itself around her like water, filling her senses. It swam around her body, wrapped its silky tendrils around her face, and blinded her completely. The sound of the sea was in her ears and she could smell and taste it; she could even feel its salt on her skin. But the dark was her ocean now, and she felt close to drowning. The inky blackness swallowed everything, making sound and taste muted and distant.

Gasping for breath, she dropped to her knees on the sandy floor of the cave. She shivered in the cool air and waved her fingers helplessly in front of her face. Not until her palm brushed her nose could she tell that her hand was there, and she closed her eyes in despair. Eyes open or closed, it didn't matter.

All that mattered right now was silence and speed. She had to find her way back to her friends. She had to do it in darkness. She had to do it in silence. Any sound she made now could betray her presence to the people outside, and all would be lost. Her friends would be gone. No one else knew where they were. No one. And the voices outside were getting closer.

She heard a cry of triumph and a hard, spiteful laugh. Conrad's voice rang out as clearly as though he were standing beside her.

"We've made it, Dad! This is the last shipment tonight, and tomorrow we'll get the cash."

She heard a slap ring out like a shot. "Keep yer voice down, and yer face shut, ya stupid idiot," the voice growled. "Nothing is over until the money is in our hands." Darrell heard another ringing smack, this time followed by the sound of something falling hard to the sand. "That'll teach ya to talk outta turn. Now get up and get to work, ya big goof." Sounds of activity came clearly though the crevice. Darrell stood up and silently crept to the back of the cave.

Remember, remember, remember, she chanted silently to herself. Reaching one arm length at a time, she felt her way along the rock wall of the cave. The night was very cool, with the thick, coppery smell of a storm in the air. In spite of the temperature, her skin burned and her body shook with exhaustion and tension. Sweat trickled behind her ears and ran down the length of her spine.

The darkness enveloped her body, but her thoughts glowed clear. Somehow, everything that had happened this summer had been because of her. Her friends had been dragged away from all they held dear, and her mistakes had led them to the brink of disappearing forever. There was no room for any more mistakes. This time, she had to do everything right.

Along the wall, her fingers brushed something — a different texture. She touched the surface lightly and something changed. She could feel electricity flowing through her body like a river and almost expected to see sparks snap from her fingertips. Instead, a strange form took shape under her fingers. A symbol that took the shape of a mask began to glow a deep, hot red on the cave wall. Relief flooded though her. Now she knew what to do.

At that very moment, she felt pressure on her leg and something cold on her back. She gasped and, in spite of herself, let out a little sob of regret. She had been caught. Her future was lost in the past.

"What...?" she cried as she was suddenly knocked backwards. Her head struck a rock outcrop painfully as she sat down hard on the sand. Darrell put up her hands to protect herself, but instead of another blow, something cool cut through the heat of the muggy night, brushing her forehead damply. A cold nose pressed against her face.

"Delaney!" Darrell nearly cried with relief. She reached out her hands and took his large head between them awash in the comfort of his presence.

Darrell heard shouts in the distance as she ruffled the dog's fur.

"I don't know how you got here, boy, but you've got to sit, Delaney," Darrell whispered in the dog's ear.

"Be a good boy, just sit here and stay quiet." Delaney obediently flopped down on the sand beside Darrell, but as soon as she took her hands off his head and turned to touch the wall, he held up a paw as it if it were sore and began to whine.

To her horror, Darrell heard the distant sound of voices, echoing off the walls of the cave. *Conrad!* But how could he have found the entrance in the dark?

"Delaney," she whispered frantically, "Delaney, please be quiet!" Outside the cave, the voices, though still distant, fell suddenly silent, as though listening. Far behind her, the walls of the cave took on a flickering glow.

Her heart pounding with fear, she curled the fingers of one hand through Delaney's fur. She tucked the book under her arm and resolutely slid her other hand along until the smoothness of the glyphs slid under her fingertips. Her fingers traced the shape of the mask, and the glyph began to glow. As the whirlwind pulled her in, she thought she heard voices calling behind her and the bark of a dog.

CHAPTER FOURTEEN

Darrell lay on the sand, sick and miserable. Her head was spinning and her stomach roiling, and when she should be ready to jump into the fray and rescue her friends, all she wanted to do was sleep and make it all go away. She felt for her pocket in the dark and found a peppermint to slip into her mouth.

Finally sitting up after her nausea began to ebb, she leaned against a wall and thought how much easier the recovery was with the candy in her mouth. *It must have to do with blood sugar or something like that.* Her eyes were drawn to the shape of the mask on the rock wall, glowing red in the centre and charred around the edges. She could no longer see the sword-shaped glyph, as it was now most certainly completely blackened. Now that she was here, all the certainty she had in her plans for saving her friends melted away.

Standing up on shaky legs, Darrell slowly felt her way to the front of the cave, then dropped to her hands and knees to creep out to look at the sky. The sun was setting. A crisp breeze floated in through the entrance and she shivered and moved back inside. Autumn was coming, she could smell it. A pinkish light crept through the entrance of the cave, not much to see by, but at this point, all the light she really needed.

She peeked up into the rock ledge that was tucked inside the entrance to the cave. It had been swept clean of all it had held before. The tide was out, but the sand on the floor of the cave still felt damp under her woollen skirt. How could two men have sheltered in that tiny space, particularly when one was the size of Sir William? At the thought of the giant Scot, Darrell's heart gave a lurch. How had he fared in the skirmish with Hamish and his men? Had he really been struck down immediately? There was so much she didn't know.

Whatever had happened, she would have to be very careful. She bit her lip and sat down to take stock of the precious items with which she had filled her pockets before leaving. She pulled everything out of her pockets into a pile on the sand and then picked them up one by one. For the first time since she had arrived in the cave, she smiled, looking at the changes that the journey through time had made. Her library book was a roll of parchment, tied with ribbon. She unrolled it and glanced quickly at the words it contained, now written in Latin, outlining the need for basic personal hygiene and household cleanliness to prevent disease. The wax of the plain white candle she had pulled from her bedside table was now yellow, and it felt greasy in her hands. And the Swiss army knife she had taken from Lily's bedside table now took the form of a slim dagger, sheathed in leather. She shuddered a bit, thinking of Hamish, and hoped she would not have to use it.

Her shoe was now soled with wood, like a clog, but with a full leather upper. She pulled up the hem of her dress, smiling again slightly as she noticed Eleanor's mending, and carefully unwrapped her leg and checked the padding she had applied in her room at school. The soft pad of cotton remained unchanged, except now it looked more like a linen material. She carefully replaced it between her leg and the wooden peg, to give the most cushioning possible and to help ease the soreness.

Well, she thought, *this is as ready as I will ever be.* She was pocketing all the items when she realized with a shock that Delaney had not appeared. She sat back on her heels. Delaney had whimpered as she had been yanked through the wall of time. He had been her guide on every journey. This time, had she left him to the mercy of Conrad and his father? Her throat tightened. If anything happened to the dog, she would never forgive herself.

She sat by the mouth of the cave and watched the sun set over the Scottish highlands in a blaze of glory. "I'll just wait until it gets a little darker and then make my way around the path by candle light," she whispered. She pulled the candle from her pocket and then realized with a groan that she had not brought matches to light it. "They probably wouldn't have made it through the journey anyway," she muttered. "I think they still use flint to light fires here." She thought the matter over quickly. The lack of a light might actually work to her advantage. Travelling at night was never very safe, and she knew that most honest people usually went to bed with the sun. She would need to be very careful to avoid anyone on the road to the castle.

As dusk settled all around, Darrell stood up and started out of the cave. In spite of the twilight, she remembered the way, and if she kept to the road it would lead her directly to Ainslie Castle on the tidal island.

As she walked, the moon rose over the ocean and she was able to make her way up with comparative ease to the road that ran along the ridge. She found herself making better time than she had thought, for the road was deeply rutted, but it was dry and she managed to pick her way through the worst of the dips and dents with relative ease, teetering just a bit on her wooden leg.

Soon Darrell was in sight of the castle, standing below it on the road that led to the small tidal island.

She glanced up at the moon and saw that it had travelled quite a distance across the night sky. It stood over the craggy hills of the western highlands. What she could not see was how clearly it backlit her figure as she limped slightly on the road to the castle.

She was midway on her journey up from the beach when she heard hoof-beats rising up to her ears from the direction of Ainslie. She looked around in dismay, seeing little protection or cover in which to hide. Too late she realized that the foliage around this road was kept deliberately scant to prevent ambush.

She watched helplessly as two horsemen rode swiftly up the hill. Her heart began to pound again with the sound of the hooves. She looked frantically for someplace to hide, but they were upon her less than a minute after she had first heard the sound of the hooves. A voice thundered out:

"Who walks these perilous roads unaccompanied in the dark of night?"

Darrell peered up at the dark-shrouded faces of the horsemen.

"It is only I, Dara of — of Eagle Glen, returning to the home of my host."

The second horseman gave a strangled cry and jumped off his horse. Before he could say a word, the first horseman spoke up again.

"God be praised!"

Darrell was flooded with relief as she saw it was Luke who smiled down at her. She teetered on her feet and took a step backwards so as to not fall down with sheer relief.

"This is wonderful news, Dara. Sir William and the Lady Eleanor have been sick with yer loss. Some items of yers were found near the body of Hamish in the cave. Father and I feared the worst."

"The *body* of Hamish..." repeated Darrell, dazedly.

"There is much that has happened in yer absence, Dara," said Luke. "Let us return to the castle and all will be known." He turned his horse and called to his second. "Give the lady a hand to help her up on the horse. Ye can ride behind her."

Darrell turned and found herself looking into the twinkling eyes of Brodie.

"Your foot, wee lassie," he said, smiling, and swung her gently up onto the back of the horse.

The wind had started to blow in earnest as they thundered down the hill. Though Brodie hung on to her steadily, Darrell still spent most of the ride with her eyes tightly closed. He seemed confident, but Darrell was fairly sure that Brodie was as much a city kid as herself. And he had probably ridden as many horses before this journey started as she had — meaning none. Darrell didn't open her eyes until they were stopped at the castle gate. She looked up and could see the openings above the gate that the guards called down through. When Luke called up that all was well, the portcullis was drawn up and the enormous wooden doors opened to let them in.

Sir William was in the entrance to meet them and reached up to sweep Darrell off the horse. She found herself wrapped in his embrace and then he quickly stepped back and took her by the shoulders.

"Words cannot say how glad I am to see ye returned safely to us. Are ye well?"

Darrell looked back at him dumbly. She had thought she would have the whole evening to prepare a story to cover her absence, but being found so early meant that she didn't even know how much time had passed since she had been gone, let alone come up with a story about where she had been.

Brodie spoke up. "It is as we had thought, Sire. She relayed the story to me on our return. After the battle, she swooned and was captured by thieves. They plundered the cave and stole her away. She was only able to make her escape this evening, while they slept, overcome with the mead they had drunk."

Sir William clutched Darrell's arms in his huge hands. "Are these words true, my dear? And are ye completely unharmed?"

KC DYER

Darrell glanced gratefully at Brodie. "Indeed, Sir William, my servant speaks the truth. I am safe and glad to be back under your protection."

"Then our sorrow for yer fate has turned to joy." He turned to a serving woman, standing nearby. "Maggie, take the Lady to her chamber with Lady Eleanor, and be sure to shake Eleanor awake so she can share in the joyful news." He turned to Darrell, laughing. "She is a sound sleeper, my girl Ellie. If she cannot be woken, I am sure she will dream of our good luck in finding ye safe and having ye back with us once again."

Darrell felt quite overwhelmed by the kind reception she had received, but she was filled with questions.

"I am so grateful for your kindness, Sir William. Thank you for your hospitality and your protection. But before I go up to my roo — solar, please spare me a few moments to talk with my treasured servant Brodie."

"Indeed, lass. If ye are in need of refreshment, please hasten to the kitchens, where Maggie will provide all that ye need."

After another flurry of bowing and thanks, Brodie and Darrell managed to make their way to the kitchen. They sat at a large table that doubled as a preparation place for the household meals and spoke quietly while Maggie provided them with bread and cheese. To Maggie's amusement, they refused mead and took cider to drink instead. As Darrell sat down she heard a sharp bark, and a moment later a brown dog put his head in her lap.

"Delaney!" Releif flooded through her at the sight of the dog, safe in the warm kitchen. He licked her face and held up his paw. She looked at it anxiously.

"It's much better," said Brodie. "I don't think it was broken, just a bad strain. He limps a bit, but he's getting better, right, boy?" Brodie patted Delaney's head, fondly.

"Join the club, Delaney,' said Darrell, rubbing her sore leg. "Limping must be catching, lately."

Maggie left the kitchen, but they continued to speak in whispers so as not to be overheard.

"Thanks for the cover story, Brodie. So much has happened and I didn't know what to say to Sir William."

"I could see how you might be stuck. I knew you'd be back, so I worked that story out just in case."

"How long have I been gone?" asked Darrell in a low voice.

"Five days." Brodie's eyes were shining. "I am so glad you are back. We were very worried, and after we catch up here, we've got to go and find Kate."

"Where is she?"

"I'm not sure. When you were gone that morning, they all blamed her for not keeping you safe."

Darrell looked horrified. "Has she been punished?"

Brodie looked uncomfortable. "Not punished, real-ly. They just made her feel terrible, and she has been made to work very hard while you have been gone." He paused, seeing Darrell's stricken face. "I did have a chance to talk with her a bit, and she is mostly worried about you. So tell me, what really happened after all?"

Darrell quickly related the story of the Hamish and his murderous intentions.

"So the last thing that happened that I remember slashing his hand and hearing a shout. Delaney and I ran like crazy, but I fell and hit the wall and it sent me back through to the cave near the school." She paused for breath. "I didn't see anyone else, though. I can't believe that Hamish tried to kill me and now he is dead."

Brodie sipped his cider. "I can tell you what happened. Apparently Hamish had been romancing Eleanor since Sir William left. He was collecting a group of soldiers and buying their loyalty with privi-leges and favours. Anyway, he thought he had enough support to rise up against Sir William, but he hadn't counted on Luke.

"What do you mean?"

"He means that I knew what he was planning all along." Luke walked in through the doorway from the stables and poured himself a cup of mead. "My da is a fine fisherman, and when he left our family to find a safe place in the north, he managed to catch himself a really big fish while he was at it." He grinned and sat down beside Darrell.

Darrell smiled. "Sir William?" she guessed.

"That's right. Sir William was on his way back from meeting with his relatives amongst the Norse. The plague had spread there as well, so he was returning home when his ship foundered against some rocks in the Orkneys. My da was sailing home on his return journey and he spotted seals on the rocks. Turned out to be Sir William and his last man. The others had all drowned, and Sir William and his man were weak and sick. The man died on the trip back, but my da managed to nurse Sir William back to health. They came ashore one day while I was alone on patrol." He grinned at the memory. "I told Sir William of the growing insurrection, so we decided that I would test the loyalty of the soldiers."

Brodie laughed. "From stable boy to soldier in twenty-four hours." He looked at Luke. "Turns out that most of the group that were loyal to Hamish were not even members of the regular guard. Hamish had been handing out commissions as favours. In the face of Sir William and his loyal troops, Hamish and his group were crushed."

Luke sat down at the table and smiled grimly. "D'ye ken the look on my da's face when Hamish tried to stab Sir William when his back was turned battling two others?" He pulled his own slim knife from inside his stocking and laid it gently on the table.

Brodie nodded. "I thought the veins would pop out of his head, he was so furious." He looked at Darrell, his eyes clouded with the memory. "I've never seen anything like it. Most of the time I spent trying to keep my back to the rocks and away from all the weaponry." He eyed Luke's knife warily, as though it might jump from the table of its own accord and turned back to Darrell. "I didn't know who was fighting on which side ... just man against man, sword against shield. The noise was deafening ..."

"Until the blows began to hit home," Luke concluded quietly. "A broadsword against flesh makes a sound so silent it could deafen ye."

Brodie nodded and swallowed. "I didn't hear the sound of Hamish's death," he said quietly. "I just saw him slide off the end of your father's blade."

Darrell blanched. If it hadn't been for her, Brodie would never been at risk in the sudden battle. He had seen someone die violently before his eyes ... something she was grateful to have missed. So much had happened in so short a time. Hamish gone, the rebellion quashed, and both Luke and Eleanor had their fathers back again.

Luke smiled warmly and patted Darrell's arm. "I'm off to bed, lass. I've early duty in the morning." He slipped his knife back into his stocking and disappeared into the darkness outside the kitchen door.

Darrell still felt a bit dizzy. "Thanks for all the news, Luke. See you in the morning." She turned to Brodie as Luke left the kitchen. "I'm sorry you had to see all that, Brodie." She smiled wryly. "I guess you're a soldier now, are you? You may get to like it here and never want to return to the humdrum life of Eagle Glen."

"Well, I wouldn't exactly call it ..."

"DARRELL!"

Darrell just had time to stand up when she felt like she had been hit by a freight train. Kate ran in and picked her right up off her feet, hugging Darrell so tightly she could hardly speak.

"I am glad to see you, too, Kate," Darrell said, breathlessly.

Tears were running down Kate's face. Brodie pulled a small stool up to the table, and Kate sat down. Maggie, who had found Kate and brought her to the kitchen, smiled sleepily and headed back to her interrupted night's rest.

Kate caught her breath and looked at Darrell. "I thought we would never get to go home again," she said with a sniff. "What happened, Darrell? How could you leave us like that?"

Darrell told the story to Kate once again, with Brodie interjecting at intervals with details.

Kate put her face in her hands and sighed. "Everyone was so angry with me for letting you go somewhere unattended."

"I wasn't!" Brodie interjected.

"Everyone except Brodie," Kate corrected herself. "He believed whatever had happened, if we were patient, you would show up." She looked at Brodie. "I guess you were right, after all. Anyway, I have had to work so hard this week while you have been gone. I thought my back would break!" She smiled ruefully. "At first I thought they were punishing me, but after a couple of days I realized that this is the way everybody works. It made my tae kwon do training look like a picnic."

Brodie nodded. "I have been grateful for my Scottish grandmother, though," he said with a grin. The girls looked at him in surprise. "How do you think I got named Broderick?" he said, sheepishly. "It sounds just right when these Ainslie people say it with that Gaelic burr." He puffed out his chest, imitating the head horseman. "Brrrrodie, me lad, toss me that bale o' hay. Brrrrodie, just unsaddle and groom these sixteen horses before mid-day, there's a good man."

Kate and Darrell laughed, and Kate held up her red hands for the others to see.

"You think you've had it bad. These hands have scrubbed the stones in the scullery every day and washed all the clay pots and plates after every meal. I'll be glad to go back to just being your maid for a while, Darrell." She laughed again. "Just don't expect it when we get back to Eagle Glen."

Darrell looked serious. "We have to decide what we are going to do next. I've got a couple of things to do before we go, but I think we have to try to get back at the soonest opportunity. We can't run the risk of one of us getting hurt or kidnapped again."

Brodie spoke up. "I've got an idea. Everyone in this place seems very religious. I know there is a small church in the village. I think we need to pretend we are going there to offer thanks for Darrell's safe return, and then head back to the cave."

"That's a great idea," Darrell grinned. "The little church down in the village is close enough that Sir William will not feel he has to send us with a big entourage and we can quickly zip to the beach and find the cave." She paused for a moment. "We have to make sure Delaney is with us," she added thoughtfully. "He has been with me on every trip through time … and I think he really has to be there for us to make the journey home."

"Okay, that's settled." Kate's head drooped with fatigue. "Now, I need to get some sleep. They've been waking me up at four in the morning to light the fires." She smiled at Darrell. "Now that I can return to my pallet in Eleanor's room, I might get to sleep until six!"

They said goodnight, and the girls made their way up the darkened stairs to Eleanor's room. Brodie and Delaney and walked out through the back of the kitchen to their beds in the stables.

The next morning after eating, Darrell made her case with Sir William. He was readying his horsemen to make a round of his lands, gathering tithes and food-stuffs for the coming winter. While he was away, he and his men would hunt for meat to store in the cold cellars of the kitchen at Ainslie Castle. A few of his trusted sol-diers would remain behind to protect the castle, led by the now-favoured Luke Iainson. He was delighted that his fine Lady Dara wanted to visit a church that was under his protection and when she assured him that she would be safe, agreed to send only two guards.

Their plans in place, Darrell went upstairs to Lady Eleanor's solar. She found Eleanor with her maids, sit-ting on the cushioned seat by the window, stitching diligently. She had seemingly recovered quickly from the loss of Hamish's favours and was giggling with her maids about the brilliant blue eyes of the new captain of the guard.

Darrell sat down beside Eleanor on the window seat. "Lady Eleanor," she began carefully, "as mistress of Ainslie Castle, does any of the care of the sick fall to you?"

Eleanor nodded. "I am often called upon to help bind up the wounded or to try to treat the sick." She sighed. "Ernestina and I labour together in this regard. I can help her, for though I am less skilled, I can read what few words we have that are written in instruction. It is a hard and thankless task, and many who are ill go quickly to their place in heaven." She looked at Darrell sadly. "Is it not so at yer home, Lady Dara?"

Darrell nodded, then decided to change the subject. "I have a gift for you, Lady Eleanor." She produced the rolled parchment from her pocket and handed it to Lady Eleanor.

Eleanor looked surprised and pleased. Before she could speak, Darrell said, "It is a gift to thank you and your family for your kind hospitality."

Eleanor looked at her, puzzled. "Ye sound as though ye are planning to leave."

"Oh no!" replied Darrell hastily. "Not at all. It's just — well, I am very worried about the Black Death that has swept though your land. I think this book — er — this parchment will give you some idea about how to keep well the people under your care. Your interest in keeping the floors clean is important — and perhaps stabling all the animals outside will reduce the fleas."

Eleanor started to untie the ribbon on the scrolled parchment.

"No need to look at it now," Darrell said hastily. "Please just remember that clean bodies and rooms make it harder for the disease to spread." Eleanor nodded and spread her arms wide to hug Darrell.

"Thank ye for thinking of us," she said quietly. "I look forward to learning more of yer ideas this evening, when ye return from the church."

Darrell nodded, and she and Kate left the solar. They quickly ran down the stone spiral staircase and met Brodie in the stables, waiting patiently with a dirty brown dog.

Sir William had already left when they made their way down to the village in the carriage that he insisted they take. It was a simple matter to ask for a walk along the beach before they made their pilgrimage to the church. The guards remained with the carriage as lookouts for potential trouble, and Darrell, Brodie, Kate, and Delaney made their way carefully down the sandy path to the beach.

Brodie looked back up the hill at their protectors and saw that one guard had already nodded off, while the other leaned, head on his hands, staring off into the distance in the warmth of the late summer sun.

Brodie grinned. "I hope that Sir William is not too hard on them when he finds they have lost us again. With me out of there, they will definitely need an extra hand at cleaning out the stables."

Darrell looked around wistfully. "We have been so lucky," she said, "to be able to see all of this for ourselves."

"I think we are lucky to live at the time we do," retorted Kate. "These people lived very hard, short lives. It was lucky their religion gave them some comfort, because they had to work so hard just to survive."

They stepped in through the entrance to the cave. The summer sun shone through the opening but they lit candles to find their way to the back of the cave. In the flickering light, they could see the remaining symbol on the cave wall. The mask was blackened around the edges but began to glow a deep ochre red as they stepped closer.

Brodie knelt down and gave a last pat to the dirty brown dog. "You have been great company, Delaney. I'm glad your paw is almost better."

Kate turned to Darrell. "Have you got the mints?" Darrell nodded. "I'm going to close my eyes, then. I am not looking forward to this!" She reached out and grabbed Darrell with one hand and Brodie with the other.

On the hillside above them, they could hear shouts as the guards discovered their absence.

"I sure hope this works," said Darrell. Brodie grasped her shoulder with his free hand and Darrell curled her fingers through Delaney's soft fur and touched the glowing mask on the wall.

Chapter Fifteen

Darrell, winded, still managed to be the first to sit up. She propped herself against the wall, and some colour returned to her face. She watched Kate shake her head, like a dog just coming out of the water, and heave herself onto her knees. Brodie was still out cold, with his hair sticking straight up and his face in the sand. She reached over and handed Kate a mint, than had one herself. She felt around and plucked a flashlight from inside Brodie's pack; the thin yellow light shone on their faces.

Kate was the first to speak.

"Well, I guess we made it back," she said faintly, spitting a few grains of sand as she spoke. She turned and looked at Brodie as he started to stir beside her on the sand. "He looks as bad as I feel," she muttered.

Darrell grinned. "You're not exactly the picture of beauty yourself." She pointed to Kate's jeans, which were ripped at the knees. "Nice pants."

Kate laughed. "This travelling is a bit rough on the clothing. I'm glad to have my jeans back after that skirt. The wool was starting to make me itch." She ran her finger along the torn line of fabric at her knee.

Brodie groaned and sat up. Darrell and Kate grinned over at him as he stretched his stiff arms and grimaced at the nausea. He looked up but couldn't quite manage to smile back.

"I guess the walking wounded have all returned, safe if not sound," he said in a low voice. Kate handed him a peppermint.

"I think it was a bit easier coming back than it was getting there," Kate said. "I don't hurt quite as much as I did the last time, and I definitely feel less sick to my stomach."

Brodie nodded. "I think you're right. The candy really seems to help. Maybe after a few dozen more trips, we'll get the hang of it."

Darrell shook her head. "You've forgotten something," she said quietly. "This is it. Tomorrow is our last day of school. Look at your watch, Brodie."

Darrell directed the beam of the flashlight and Brodie glanced down at his watch. August 21. It was nearly time to go home.

Kate jumped up. "I can't believe it! How did this summer go so fast? I'm not ready to go home — I mean, I thought I wanted to go home — but — I don't know what I want!" She burst into tears and sat back down on the sand.

Darrell crawled over and patted Kate gently on the leg. When Kate's sobs had subsided, Darrell directed the flashlight at the wall of the cave. The light cast a pale yellow glow onto the wall. The last of the symbols had faded from red to black, and the cave wall was a smooth, blank face of sandstone marred only by three charcoal smudges.

Brodie spoke up, his voice dull. "It *is* over, Kate. The symbols are gone. There is nothing left to take us back." He shrugged, and looked away from Kate, whose eyes were beginning to leak again.

Darrell sat up, adjusted her prosthesis, and retied her shoe. As she stood up, Delaney loped up to her, tail waving delightedly. He licked Kate's face as she struggled to get up and padded over to where Darrell was standing. He hopped up and planted his two big paws on her shoulders in greeting, and then spun back toward the entrance to the cave. Ears forward, tail wagging, he barked joyfully and bounded out of sight once more.

"His paw looks completely better," said Darrell. She felt relieved to see Delaney looked like he had made a full recovery, but her relief was tempered by sadness at the thought that their travels were over.

Brodie reached over and helped Kate up, and the three of them slowly slipped out of the cave.

"I guess it doesn't matter if anyone sees us," Darrell said with a sigh. She looked around sadly as they walked up the beach. Dawn was not far away. Lights shone out of the kitchen windows at the rear of the school. Exhausted from their travel through the centuries, they climbed slowly up the winding path into the garden. Delaney curled up in a tight ball at the base of the arbutus tree and closed his eyes.

"I guess we all need some sleep," Brodie said, nodding at the dog as he slipped in through the back door. "Good night, you two."

"More like good morning," muttered Kate as she and Darrell headed for the stairs.

The next thing Darrell knew she was being violently shaken up and down.

"Hey! Leave me alone! What's happening?" she cried.

"Wake up, Darrell! I have to talk to you RIGHT NOW!"

Darrell opened her eyes blearily to find Lily Kyushu staring into her face.

"I have news!" she said, excitement in every word. "It started last night and I tried to find you and Kate, but you were nowhere to be found." She paused for breath. "Where were you, anyway? *I* wasn't going to tell on you but Andrea was worried and she told Professor Tooth, and with all the excitement and police cars and everything I thought she would freak out but she was really calm and anyway if you don't hurry up, you're going to miss it!" For emphasis, she jumped up and down a few more times on Darrell's bed.

Kate sat up, her red hair pointing straight at the ceiling, both front and back. She looked furious.

"Lily, would you SHUT UP? Darrell and I didn't get to bed until very late, early this morning really, and we need to sleep. So just GO AWAY, at least for a few more hours." She lay back down and pulled the pillow over her head.

Darrell looked sleepily at Lily. "Normally, I would agree wholeheartedly with Kate, but did you say *police*?"

Lily looked smug. "Yes I did, and it is all because of me that they're here."

Darrell sat up blearily and groped for her prosthesis. "Okay," she said. "You'd better tell me the whole story."

Lily giggled. "Throw on a coat, you guys. I'll tell you everything I know on the way down."

Darrell hauled Kate out of bed, and the two girls grabbed their coats to cover their pyjamas. They followed Lily down to the back garden, all thoughts of sleep forgotten. Many of the students were standing in the garden, staring down at the action unfolding on the beach. Lily waved at a police officer standing near the arbutus tree, and the officer walked up to Darrell.

"Are you Darrell Connor? I'm Special Constable Rene Arseneault. Please follow me."

Darrell raised her eyebrows at Lily and Kate as they trailed behind the police officer. The sky was clear but there was an ominous line of clouds scudding across the horizon. The air smelled of salt borne on the wind. They made their way down the winding path from the school to the beach. Though the constable was silent, Lily chattered the whole way down.

"Remember when I told you that Conrad Kennedy had been buzzing by me in his boat? Well, it turns out that he wasn't just poaching crabs but he was smuggling, too!"

"Oh, yeah," said Darrell. "Smuggling."

"You don't look very surprised."

"Ah — that's just because — ah — I'm sleepy." Darrell tried to think more clearly. "Smuggling," she said again. "I can't believe it!"

Kate spoke up. "Oh, so those white plastic boxes *were* his, then."

Lily looked with a confused expression between Kate and Darrell. "How much do you guys know about this, anyway?"

Darrell shot Kate a warning glance. "Nothing, Lily, really nothing at all. It's just that you mentioned the boxes when you were bouncing on my bed to wake me up. Kate must have heard you say it then."

Kate agreed hurriedly. "That's it, exactly Lily. I just heard you before."

Lily looked puzzled. "I'm sure I didn't say anything like that. How ..." she interrupted herself with a shout. "Look! There's Conrad Kennedy on the beach."

Still following the police officer, Darrell, Kate, and Lily made it down to the small cove near the rock face and the entrance to the cave. Constable Arseneault turned to Darrell.

"I believe you made a report earlier this summer with regard to illegal crabbing activities on this beach?"

Darrell nodded. "That's right. Only, I didn't actually make the report. It was my teacher, Mr. Gill. He promised to look into it for me."

A roar filled the air. "Let me go! You've got the wrong guy, all right? Watch what you're doing!"

Darrell looked up to see Conrad Kennedy being escorted off a small boat pulled up on shore. The police were having some difficulty getting him to walk up the beach. From the loud banging and crashing noises on the boat, there was clearly a struggle taking place in the small cabin of the craft as well.

Police officers finally managed to place handcuffs on Conrad and they walked him along the shore away from the boat, which now was rocking from side to side on the beach. Conrad caught sight of Darrell.

"Hey, Gimpy! I'm going to set the record straight with these guys. You're the one they want, not me. All I've done is catch a few crabs. You're the one who's always snooping around down here." He turned to the officer escorting him. "The boxes you found don't belong to us, sir. That girl is always down here snooping around. They must be hers."

There was a resounding crash from the ship and suddenly a man leapt through a window of the small cabin, shattering the glass. He rolled on the sand and to his feet in one smooth motion. He pelted up the shore-line at top speed, heading right for the spot where Darrell stood with Lily and Kate.

"Get down!" shouted Constable Arseneault to the girls.

Conrad started yelling too. "Dad! DAD! Don't leave me here, Dad! C'mon, Dad, wait for me!" He jumped to his feet but was quickly subdued by two large police officers.

Conrad's father, ignoring the calls of his son, eas-ily leapt over a log and continued to flee up the beach.

He made a move to run past the girls, when Kate stepped forward.

"Going somewhere?" she said, and touched his sleeve.

The next moment, he was on the ground with both Darrell and Kate sitting on his legs. Constable Arseneault pulled his arms behind his back and snapped on the cuffs she carried. She turned to Kate.

"That was a very dangerous thing to do." Her hat had blown off in the chase and a wisp of hair blew into her eyes. "But thank you all the same," she smiled. Two other officers hustled Mr. Kennedy over to where Conrad was sitting on the beach. Before anyone knew what was happening, Mr. Kennedy started to kick Conrad in the head and torso. He was swearing and spitting like a snake.

"This is all your fault, you miserable idiot! This is what I get for trusting a baby like you to do a man's job!" He managed to land another kick before the police officers got him down to the ground. They clipped his legs in irons, and the drama was over.

Kate looked at Constable Arseneault. "What is in those boxes? Illegal drugs? Laundered money? What?"

"It *seems* to be computer parts and software."

"Really?" Kate brightened up. "What kind of parts? IBMs, Hewlett Packards, IMacs?"

Constable Arseneault smiled grimly. "I think I heard them say Atari."

Kate began to laugh. "And the software?"

"Reader Rabbit, I think."

Kate doubled over laughing, clutching her coat to cover her pyjamas.

Lily frowned. "What's so funny, Kate?"

Kate sat down on the sand, laughing hysterically. "Conrad was smuggling outdated game sets and," more peals of laughter, "educational software!"

Constable Arseneault raised her hand. "It may not be as funny as you think," she said quietly. "Those game packages were empty of games, but stuffed with heroin. And not only that, there is some evidence of human smuggling as well. Your classmate and his father have a lot to answer for."

Darrell spoke up. "He's not our classmate, officer. He just lives nearby."

Constable Arseneault nodded and jotted a few words in her notebook.

Lily frowned again. "Conrad must have been watching the beach when he was buzzing me while I was swimming!"

"Probably so. Thank you all for your help." Constable Arseneault nodded politely and walked across the beach to join the other police officers.

Darrell shook her head. "No wonder Conrad is

KC DYER

such a bully," she said. "With a father like that, anyone would have a problem."

"Yeah," Lily agreed. "The policeman I spoke to said his father would probably go to jail and Conrad will get sent to a special school. He will have to go and live with his mom anyway, and she lives in Ontario."

"Well," said Kate, still grinning, "I guess that's the last we'll see of him. It's too bad, in a way. I really enjoyed practicing tae kwon do with him." She chuckled. "His dad was pretty good at it, too."

They looked back to the shore, where three police officers each escorted Conrad and his father up to the squad cars parked in the driveway of the school. Conrad's father was still spitting and swearing as they carried him up, but Conrad, who had been allowed to walk, turned and looked back at Darrell. His face was livid. He didn't say a word, but bared his teeth and turned away.

After breakfast, Darrell, Kate, and Brodie walked down the hall, looking worn and tired. Mr. Gill stepped out of the office and caught sight of them.

"Ah, just the people I have been looking for," he said warmly. "Darrell, Brodie, Kate, could you come into my office for a moment, please?" Brodie and Darrell exchanged startled glances as they followed Kate into Mr. Gill's office. Kate glanced back at them in alarm. Had they been seen on their return this morning? Brodie shrugged one shoulder at the question in Darrell's eyes. What did it matter now, even if they had been seen? Summer school was over. This afternoon they would pack the last of their things and tomorrow was the day to go home.

Mr. Gill turned smoothly to Darrell. "I want to thank you for completing your self-portrait, Darrell." His eyes twinkled. "I do believe you have successfully emulated the style of a somewhat well-known aritist ... Leonardo da Vinci, if I am not mistaken?"

Darrell coloured a little and ducked her head to hide her smile.

"And now I believe there is a telephone call for you, Darrell. You can take it right there." He gestured at a telephone on the desk. "And if you two could join me in here, we can have a little discussion."

Brodie and Kate stepped into the inner office. Mr. Gill closed the door behind them. Darrell picked up the phone.

After Darrell's brief conversation with her mother to set up a time for the next day's pick-up, she turned away from Mrs. Follett's desk to look for Brodie and Kate, but the door to the inner office was open.

"They must have left to do their packing," she muttered to herself. She wandered outside, not able to face anyone in her present, bleak state of mind. She glanced down at the concrete slab in the garden, thinking with some surprise that she hadn't done her morning endurance test for more than half the summer.

"I guess I forgot," she muttered out loud. "Or maybe I just don't need to prove anything to myself anymore."

Darrell walked over to the arbutus tree in the garden and opened her now tattered notebook. She looked at the question she had written in bold letters after the return from her first journey.

If somehow I am able to travel through time,
Could I go back to when I was ten and prevent the accident?

What if that was really what this whole summer had been about? What if she could somehow change things so that she once again had two strong legs and a father who loved her? Darrell's mouth formed a grim line. She started down the winding path to the beach, determined to find the answer, once and for all.

CHAPTER SIXTEEN

Darrell strode down the beach with the wind swirling her brown hair as a late summer storm blew down through the fjord. She stopped in surprise to see Delaney lying on the sand, looking out over the stormy water. She followed his gaze and noticed with a start that the shattered driftwood log that had been his shelter had been drawn back out to sea by the waves. The salt spray stung her eyes, but Darrell sat down beside Delaney to watch the log drift away. She picked up a stick and traced patterns in the wet sand. The tide was going out, and because of the white-peaked waves that crashed against the shore, she could soon barely see the log, bobbing distantly among the whitecaps of the bay.

Darrell looked down and saw she had sketched the outline of a fishing boat on the sand. It looked a little like the boat that belonged to Conrad Kennedy's father. She and Delaney had walked back down to the beach after Conrad and his father had been taken away and watched a police tugboat haul the boat off the sand and chug down the fjord toward Vancouver with the small fishing vessel in tow. She had smiled as it shrank away to a tiny dot on the horizon, thinking of another small boat that had borne a cargo not of smuggled goods but of hope, in the form of two strong men who had fought the sea and won.

Darrell kicked sand over the outline and shook her head, thinking about Luke and Conrad, and the choices they had made for and because of their families. She stood up and threw the stick for Delaney. He chased it down and shook it violently, snapping it in two. Job done, he trotted back up the beach to Darrell.

The log was gone. Darrell and Delaney wandered down toward the cave and slipped through the crevice in the rock wall. Inside, she switched on her flashlight right away since the grey day meant very little light crept through the crack in the rocky roof. She wasn't worried about meeting anyone. Kate and Brodie must both be up in their rooms, packing their bags to return home for the few short days before school began again in the city. And of course Conrad Kennedy was gone for good.

And if he's not gone for good, at least he's gone for now, she thought.

After the now familiar walk to the rear of the cave, she trained the beam of her flashlight on the images on the wall. They were blackened and smudged, and it was hard to see the shapes they once took. The oak tree, the sword, the mask. Just the three symbols, nothing more. She put her hand up to touch them. Was there a trace of warmth under her fingers?

She swallowed and reached into her pocket to pull out a piece of red chalk. Holding the flashlight in her left hand she began to draw. She quickly sketched two figures, standing hand in hand beside a motorbike with a flat tire. Her fingers were shaking, so the sketch was not one of her best. She placed a trembling hand on the drawing, tucked the flashlight under her arm, and reached down to pat Delaney.

Her head began to spin and her heart leapt in her chest. She felt dizzy and staggered, and her hand slipped off Delaney's head. Her flashlight fell and she turned quickly, bumping her head sharply against an outcropping of rock. She slid to the ground, eyes open in the dark, and felt Delaney sit beside her and rest his head on her knee.

She reached her hand out, felt for the flashlight, and leaned her head back against the wall. The tears that she never let anyone see welled up in her eyes.

"I thought I could go back just one last time, Delaney. To stop him from getting on that motorcycle. To make it run out of gas. To hide his helmet so we couldn't ride. Anything, just to somehow change what happened that day." She sniffed and wiped at her eyes slowly. "I guess some things just can't be changed." She stood up and turned, miserable, to head back to the school.

As she turned, a glimmer caught the corner of her eye. She looked up suddenly and nearly jumped out of her skin. Professor Myrtle Tooth stood in front of her.

"Hello, Darrell." The calm voice echoed in the cavern that surrounded them.

"Professor Tooth! You nearly scared me to death. How did you know about this cave?"

Professor Tooth smiled. "This has been a favourite spot of mine for many years. I'm pleased that you have been able to enjoy the use of it this summer, too." She paused, and her clear, green eyes looked directly into Darrell's. "I thought it was time we had a little conversation, and this is a good place to do it. Shall we make our way forward to the cave entrance?" She reached up and touched one of the dark smudges on the wall with a smile and then turned on her heel and headed for the entrance.

Darrell followed the principal, wiping her eyes with the back of her hand, her melancholy mood replaced by puzzlement. They walked to the entrance of the cave, Professor Tooth setting a brisk pace in the dark. The light of Darrell's flash showed the principal was wearing walking shorts and sturdy boots, and she sat comfortably down on the sand near the entrance. Delaney plopped down beside her and placed his head on her knee. She patted him fondly.

"His tree-stump shelter just got pulled off the beach by the tide," said Darrell, feeling unaccountably sad.

Professor Myrtle Tooth's eyes pierced through the gloom of the cave. "Time passes," she said quietly. "And sad things happen. But life does find a way of marching on."

Darrell looked at her, puzzled. "What did you want to talk to me about, Professor Tooth?"

The principal smiled. "Did you have a good summer here, Darrell?"

Darrell nodded. "I'm very sorry it's over," she said, sadly.

"Darrell, one thing you should have learned this summer is that things are not always as they appear."

"Well," said Darrell slowly, "I did learn that. But how did you know ...?"

Professor Tooth laughed. "You would be surprised what can be learned by running an — unusual — school such as this one." She paused. "I have some news for you, Darrell, although I am not completely sure what you will think of it."

Darrell waited.

"Our school has been granted a small accredited extension. We will be accepting a few new students in the fall."

Darrell looked surprised. "Accepting new students…? You mean you'll run classes like any normal school?"

Professor Tooth shook her head with a smile. "You, of all people Darrell, should know that Eagle Glen is not like any *normal* school. But yes, we will continue to operate as an Alternative School."

"The Eagle Glen Alternative School." Darrell turned the words over on her tongue. "I kind of like the sound of that," she said. "And it sure beats the sound of my old school."

Professor Tooth stood up. "I thought it might. I believe your friends Kate and Brodie may have already been given the news." She stepped to the entrance of the cave.

"I am considering a new class," she added, with the trace of a smile, "on the history of life during the Renaissance. Michelangelo, da Vinci, Shakespeare, Christopher Wren. Such an interesting era." Her smile broadened, and her eyes gleamed in the light of the flash. "If you will forgive me a slight misquotation, *there are many more seeds of time yet to be sown*, Darrell. And now," she clicked off her flashlight, "it is time for me to move away from spelunking and toward a bit of paperwork." She turned to leave.

"Professor Tooth?"

"Yes, my dear?"

"Do you remember that lesson where you asked us what we would change from the past if we could?" Darrell cleared her throat. "Do you think it *is* possible to change things that have happened in the past? To make things turn out better, somehow? Or to stop something terrible from happening?"

Myrtle Tooth's eyes glinted in the light from Darrell's flash, but her expression was sad. "I know that terrible things happen in this world every day, Darrell. And I know that some people have the will to keep the bad from overpowering the good. In that way, they bring about change. But I couldn't tell you how it happens, or why. It just does." She paused and smiled. "When you know the right people."

She turned and slid through the crevice and out of the cave.

Darrell stared out the cave opening for a long time after Professor Tooth had walked away. Her thoughts were in a jumble. How much did Professor Tooth know about this cave and what had happened here? The way she had touched the blackened glyph, as if she knew just where it could be found on the cave wall …

A slow, strange smile began to spread across her face. She looked at Delaney.

"My mother is going to be so surprised that I want to come back here to go to school in the fall that she won't even notice if I bring home a dog." She ruffled his fur fondly. "I've got a friend, Norton, that I think you might like to meet, Delaney." She paused and picked up her things.

"Come on, boy. Let's go home." Darrell smiled her best Mona Lisa smile and, rubbing the bump on her head, followed Delaney's gently wagging tail out onto the beach.

CPSIA information can be obtained at www.ICGtesting.com
Printed in the USA
LVOW100241280613

340394LV00006B/12/P